RUNNING
THROUGH IT

LORIE SCARFAROTTI

Red Deer Press

Published in Canada by Red Deer Press, 209 Wicksteed Avenue, Unit 51, Toronto, ON M4G 0B1

Published in the United States by Red Deer Press, 311 Washington Street, Brighton, MA 02135

Red Deer Press acknowledges with thanks the Canada Council for the Arts and the
Ontario Arts Council for their support of our publishing program. We acknowledge
the financial support of the Government of Canada through the Canada Book Fund (CBF)
for our publishing activities.

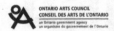 

Library and Archives Canada Cataloguing in Publication
Title: Running through it / Lorie Scarfarotti.
Names: Scarfarotti, Lorie, author.
Identifiers: Canadiana 20210395311 | ISBN 9780889956681 (softcover)
Subjects: LCGFT: Novels.
Classification: LCC PS8637.C265 R86 2022 | DDC jC813/.6—dc23

Publisher Cataloging-in-Publication Data (U.S.)
Names: Scarfarotti, Lorie, author.
Title: Running Through It / Lorie Scarfarotti.
Description: Markham, Ontario : Red Deer Press, 2022.| Summary: "Over the course of a week, thirteen-year-
old Track & Field runner, Josie Tomaselli, confronts multiple challenges with humor, confusion, fear, "lady
balls," and the inspiration of her prerace music playlist. As the big race approaches, she's missing the support
of her father, who is dying of cancer. While at first she refuses to acknowledge the possibility of losing him, in
the end she rallies to face the situation and find a way to say goodbye to her dad"-- Provided by publisher.
Identifiers: ISBN 978-0-88995-668-1 (pbk)
Subjects: LCSH Teenagers and death — Juvenile fiction. | Running for girls -- Juvenile fiction. |BISAC:
YOUNG ADULT FICTION / Sports & Recreation / Track & Field. | YOUNG ADULT FICTION / Social
Themes / Death, Grief, Bereavement.
Classification: LCC PZ7.1S337 | DDC 813.6 – dc23

Edited for the Press by Beverley Brenna
Text and cover design by Tanya Montini
Printed in Canada by Avant Imaging & Integrated Media

www.reddeerpress.com

For Shakey and my Tripod
And for all who are missed

CHAPTER 1

"RUN"

"I'm sorry I can't stay, Josie," Mom said as we pulled up next to the chain-link fence.

"I get it," I lied. The cheering echoed as the runners cruised around the royal-blue track, as if they were trying to finish before the June heat hit. The East Division Track Meet was always at one of the city high schools, and from the sound of the crowd, you'd think it was the Olympics.

"Make sure you stay hydrated."

"I know, Mom." My irritation was as subtle as her sparkly nails.

"Can't forget the lucky Mommy kiss," she said and kissed me.

"So you'll be lucky?" I smirked.

"So we'll both be. Ha! Oh, I have one from Lucas, too. Now give me your other cheek." Mom held my chin and did her wide-eyed thing that she does to look serious. "You'll do great. Be fierce!"

"You mean fearless," I said as my stomach flipped. I grabbed my bag and got out of the car.

"Same thing!" Mom giggled as I closed the door. Only it wasn't. It only highlighted that Dad wasn't going to be here. No pep talk. No thumbs-up from the stands. Mom tried, but she really didn't have a clue about running, unless she had to get out of the rain. Then she and her glittery nails would plough through anyone in her way.

As usual, my school team was in the stands by the 100-metre start line. Mr. B., our coach, went early to every track meet, just to stake out the front row, because he thought it was the prime cheering spot. He'd spread a few grubby blankets and hang our JF Penguins school banner on the railing.

"Morning, Tomaselli! You feeling speedy?" Mr. B. asked. The penguin on his black and white T-shirt looked as if it was hiding a basketball.

"You know it," I smiled, taking in the rest of his school-spirited outfit: long black shorts with a white stripe, white tube socks pulled up to his knees, black and white running shoes, and his bald head covered with a bucket hat, with penguin patches sewn all over it.

"That's the attitude that'll take you to the City Finals, kid!" he said, as he gave me my number and some pins. Mr. B. was super encouraging and probably knew, like I did, that I needed more than attitude.

After I pinned my number to my shirt, I brought my spikes and water bottle to the field outside the fence to warm up. I clicked on "Dog Days Are Over" from my playlist to help shake off the bubbling nerves. The clamour from the crowd was faint as I jogged, skipped, lunged, and stretched to the music. I'd raced the 400-metre since fourth grade, and now in eighth grade, I really didn't want this to be my last. I *had* to make the top four to move on to the City Finals, so Dad could come to that race. The only teensy-weensy problem was, I'd never made it past the East Division meet before. Minor hiccup.

The battle of the butterflies was in full swing when we were marshalled and fanned onto the track in our staggered start positions. I wiped my sweaty palms on my T-shirt, up and down along my hips, but it was the kind of wet that wouldn't dry. I was afraid I would be crap without Dad being there—like, coming last kind of crap. The doubt was doing laps in my head as I walked to lane 8. You'd think being way up front in lane 8 was a good thing, but it sucked. The girls in every other lane could see how fast I was going, but I'd have no clue about anyone else until it was too late. "Run your own race," Dad would say. His words had to be enough.

I set my starting blocks at the line and did a short practice sprint. I walked back to the blocks, and smoothed my fingers along the bumps of my French braids, my "fast hair." I took one last look at my competition. A few girls were familiar, and I figured I had a chance with them, but the ones in lanes 4 and 5 would be tough. Any runners put in 4 and 5 had the best "seed times," which meant they were the fastest. Plus, I could just tell by looking at them. One seemed calm and was lean like a whippet. I figured her stride would be so long, she'd barely touch the ground. The other girl had the strongest legs I'd ever seen—like prosciutto hanging in the deli. If we were going by legs alone, I was in a pile of trouble. Mine were like grissini—you know, those twiggy Italian breadsticks.

I did some tuck jumps to clear my head, like in "Autumnsong." I was replaying the chorus and shaking out my legs, when Ms. Starter walked across the field. Everyone knew her. She was at all our meets, and she always wore all neon, even her sunglasses and the headband that held her grey dreadlocks. The announcer's microphone crackled over the loudspeaker. "Time now ... for the Grade 8 girls ... 400-metre runners. Ms. Starter, are we ready?"

I did another quick tuck jump, before I crouched down and backed into the blocks. I put my right heel on the back pedal of the blocks and left heel on the front. I propped my thumbs and index fingers just behind the white line. The crowd quieted as Ms. Starter stepped onto the platform. I focused on the track, and imagined Ms. Starter's arm raised as she called, "Ready ... Set ..." I raised my hips. The horn blew.

It was all reflex. Butterflies blasted to feet. Legs powered. Hands sliced the air. Lane 7 girl drifted up on my left. I pushed harder and she fell back. Spikes beat the track. *Settle in.* On my left, a panting current rose around the 200-metre curve. I cranked my arms and legs. On the final curve, I felt three, or maybe four girls coming up alongside me. Sound boomed from the stands. "Be fearless," Dad's text had said. The last hundred metres. The final kick. Cheers pulsed through me. Colours blurred. Someone beside me. Prosciutto girl. Grunting, trying to take me. *No freakin' way!* I pumped my arms. Where were the others? Couldn't risk a look. Had to make City Finals. *Get there first!*

Twenty metres. Breath blasting. Chest tightening. Legs aching. *Can I do it?* I pushed my legs. Pushed the doubt. Drove harder. Prosciutto girl dropped back. I leaned hard across the finish line and—and—almost ran over the official in my lane. I staggered to a stop.

Did I win? I think I won! I actually won!

First time ever, and my parents missed it.

CHAPTER 2

"DOG DAYS ARE OVER"

So, to be clear, it was not like an Olympic kind of win, where arms are raised in victory and you wave to the cheering crowd. I wasn't sporting a flag like a cape. Not even close. I was bending over, gasping for breath. It was *that* kind of win. I couldn't even smile, because I was holding back the sour baby-barf. There would be no oatmeal-and-blueberry splatter on the track—or on my new spikes.

"Good race," Prosciutto girl said, as she tapped my shoulder and held her hand up. My legs wobbled, and I stumbled into her high-five.

"Whoa, sorry ..." I squeaked as she held me up. "Uh, thanks. You, too." I let go about a second into awkward, even though my legs still felt unstable. She was solid, and my breadsticks were about to snap.

As we congratulated each other, I imagined my parents in the stands—Dad whistling, and Mom howling and flailing her arms, like an inflatable tube person. Out of control. Still, I could've handled the embarrassment.

The officials did their official stuff, while we waited in our lanes. The other runners waved to their adoring fans, while I searched the stands for Bird, tugging my shorts out of my butt. I couldn't find her, or even Mr. B., and before I knew it, I just started waving. A subtle, Oscar-worthy wave. It was lame, but the way I saw it, having *no one* to wave to, was way worse than waving to no one.

"Great job, girls," Ms. Starter said as we were ushered off the track. I smiled. She wasn't just talking to me, but it mattered that someone had seen the race. I knew lots of kids never had anyone come watch, and they seemed to be just fine. Maybe I'd be fine, too. Maybe.

Races were nerve-racking and exhilarating, sloppy and freeing—but track season was more than that. It meant sore muscles, stinky pits, protein shakes, and runs with Dad. It meant sticking to rituals, like my pre-race playlist, French braids, and blue speckled shorts—things that never made me win, but kept me from being last. With any luck, track season meant Mom would lose her voice from cheering for every kid at my school. And track season usually ended with me clapping for other kids going to City Finals. But not this year. Track season wasn't over for me yet!

CHAPTER 3

"YOU GOTTA BE"

"Josieeee!!" Bird was leaning over the railing as I reached the stands. I jogged up the stairs, waving my ribbon as she slammed herself around me.

"You showed them those lady balls!!" Bird shook my shoulders and I soaked up her glee. She had a blue JF on one cheek, and a penguin drawn on the other. Her curly ponytail shimmied on top of her head.

"You saw me?"

"Yerp! I'd just landed my long jump, and saw the world's fastest penguin flash right by me! I was on my knees, screaming!" Bird laughed.

"Oh my God!" I shook my head, picturing her in the

sand. I should've known my best friend would've been cheering for me.

"Yeah, it was only a little embarrassing."

"So, how'd you do?" I asked.

"Fifth," she said, holding up her hand.

"That's good!"

"I should've done a leap—and worn a tutu! Oh, and maybe landed in a split!" Bird said, arms in the air like the ballerina she was. Bird was super flexible, and had been doing ballet for about as long as I'd been running. When Mr. B. saw how springy she was, he suggested she get into jumping. Bird was reluctant at first, but she got more enthusiastic when she realized she'd get to miss school. It was also a reason to wear face paint.

"Oh, hey! I got those two twins to record your race," she said, linking her arm in mine, as we walked through the fired-up crowd watching the next race.

"Two twins?" I laughed.

"Oh, shut up! Twins. Okay? Way to thank me."

"Thank you! You're the best!!"

"That's more like it," Bird said.

"I've gotta send that video to my dad."

"Oh, so does that mean Mama Lisa is here?"

"Nope. She had some big presentation."

"So ... you're sending it to your dad, but not your mom?"

"Yeah. She can wait."

"Oh, it's like that, is it?" Bird said in one of her many accents.

"Yes, it is. She wants me to text her after the race, so I will ... but she can wait for the visual."

"At least Mama Lisa is good at doing hair!" Bird said, tugging on my braid.

"I get she has to work, but I'd *never* forgive her if she didn't do my fast hair!"

"And it's working for you! Although, you could still learn to do your own fast hair," Bird teased.

■

Our team was scattered in the stands when we got back: kids and parents watching races, laughing, eating, drinking, and huddling around cell phones, and Mr. B. smack in the middle of it all.

"Hey, Tomaselli! Awesome race, kid! You eat one of these before you ran?" Mr. B. asked, holding up a hot dog.

"Eeew, no," I said, scrunching my face at both the

thought, and the relish dripping off his goatee.

"Hey, don't knock it. Makes you run on natural gas! Ha, ha!"

"Gross!" Bird and I said in unison.

"Best line of the morning. How was your jump, Viejo?"

"Not good. I came fifth."

"Oh, that's okay. You still have the triple jump. I suggest one of these for lunch," he said, as he took a massive bite.

"You know that's not even real food," Bird said. Mr. B. just chewed and rubbed his belly.

"I don't really think he cares," I said.

Kudos came my way from schoolmates, and I thanked the guys who recorded my race. They were in my grade, but I didn't know them well, except that one did hurdles and the other threw shot put. Bird and I watched the race video, and then I sent it to Dad, with the words, "Hope you're sitting down." I felt pretty witty, and when I thought about how floored he was going to be, my disappointment at him missing my event was almost gone.

Bird and I took our lunches to a shady area under some pine trees, and away from the track. Some schools had tents set up nearby, and there was a constant hum of cheering. No one else ever sat here, because of all the pine needles on the ground, but it was our spot at every track meet. I had a special red picnic blanket—waterproof on one side—and the plastic kept the needles from poking us. At cross-country meets, when it was chilly, Dad would bundle me like a cannoli, or sometimes Mom wrapped it around herself like a skirt. She could be funny at times.

Mr. B.'s disgusting hot dog didn't stop us from diving into our lunches. The food I had on race days was also part of the ritual: pasta, carrots, cucumbers, hummus, cut-up apple, and chewy granola bars. I popped a mini carrot into my mouth before opening my thermos. Fusilli with pesto and chicken.

"Can you believe you're going to Citys next week?" Bird asked, as she bit into her sandwich and bumped me with her shoulder.

"Not at all," I said, stabbing a piece of chicken with my fork.

"I don't mean it like it's unbelievable, but it's unbelievable!" she laughed. "And just so cool, because it's our last year of middle school before the big move to high school."

"I know," I said. The pasta was suddenly hard to swallow. "Makes me freaking nervous, though."

"You say it, but you never seem nervous."

"I am, though. I get so sick!" I took a sip of water. "At least it goes away once I start running."

"I get it. When I have a show, I'm afraid I'm going to forget the steps."

"But you never, ever do."

"Not yet. But the night before my show, you always get that call and have to talk me down! So, cheers to having each other's backs!" Bird held up her water bottle and I grabbed mine. As we clanked bottles, we leaned forward, and did our exaggerated stare into each other's eyes. "Cheers!" we said together.

"Speaking of cheers, we're still going to the fair this Saturday, right?" Bird asked.

"Obviously."

"Okay. Um. So ...?" Bird said, in a cartoon voice.

"So? So what?" I asked.

"Well ... should I ask my brother to get us some booze?" Bird tipped her head, and smiled the way she always did when she already knew my answer.

"You think he will? He's not old enough."

"Yeah, but he has ways." Bird smiled. Bird's brother made fun of us the few times we snuck booze from their parents' liquor cabinet. Some tasted like warm candy, others smelled so awful, we never tried them. We were *so sure* that Bird's parents marked the level of each bottle, that we only took tiny capful tasters and replaced each one with a capful of water. We lived on the edge.

"Hey! We can celebrate your big win!" Bird decided.

"Okay, now you have to make it for the triple jump!" I said.

"Well, don't get your hopes up. It's such an awkward jump." Bird popped a grape in her mouth as my phone rang, with a picture of Dad's goofy face on the screen.

"Hi, Dad!"

"Hey! Congratulations, sweetheart!"

"Thank you." I beamed at Bird.

"What a race!"

"Can you believe it?"

"Course I can! Am I going to see you later?"

"Uh-huh. Bird's doing triple jump soon," I smiled.

"Hi!!!" Bird leaned into my phone, then pecked her cantaloupe with a toothpick.

"Wish the jumping Bird good luck. Love you. *Ciao*."

"Okay. Bye, Dad." I smiled and dove back into my lunch.

CHAPTER 4

"AS"

I watched my race about a gazillion times on the subway ride to the hospital. It was definitely me running around that track, but at the same time, not me. My arms and hands were relaxed and graceful. I looked determined. Maybe even fearless.

The lobby of the hospital looked like a mini mall, with all its stores and snack bars. Once I got off the elevator on the third floor, the fluorescent lights and chemical lemon smell was all hospital. I tried breathing through my mouth on the way to Dad's room, but gave up when I started to taste chemicals. *He cannot stay here much longer,* I thought.

"Hi Daddy!" I said as I stepped into his room. Nothing had changed since he'd arrived a few days ago. Same yellow curtain blocking the door, same white blanket, same small screens and IV hanging next to him.

"Hey, there's my champ!" he smiled, putting his phone on the blanket, and reaching toward me. I gave him a kiss on the cheek. His hair smelled as oily as it looked.

"Whoa, Dad, time to wash that." I flicked my fingers near his head.

"Oh, yeah, I wanted to talk to you about my hair before we talk about the race," he said.

"Is that sarcasm?" I asked.

"You're learning! So, how many times do you think I watched your race?" he asked, lifting his phone.

"Twice?"

"Multiply it by ten. Come, sit." He patted the bed and I slid beside him, trying to ignore the way his hair stuck together, and separated in clumps to show his scalp. Even a brush might've helped. Dad tapped his phone.

"We don't need to watch it," I said, embarrassed.

"Quiet, you. This brings me joy," he said as he hit play. "Look at your great start!"

"Oh, I hated that lane!"

"And, you dealt with it. Look how strong you are along the back stretch. Beautiful. Like it's easy."

"Didn't feel easy."

"Ha! It's not supposed to. Oh! I love this ... you girls coming around the last curve ... synchronized." He pointed to the screen, and I scooched in to watch again.

"And ... there's the kick!!" Dad chuckled, his eyes widening. I'd never seen Dad's face when I raced, but maybe this is how he always looked. I felt his pride in my stride. "You really killed it, Jose." He kissed my head. "So? Tell me, how were the nerves?"

"Fine." I got off the bed and moved to the chair.

"Really?" he asked, like he didn't buy it. Sometimes I just wanted to leave it at "fine," but both my parents always liked to *talk* about things. The nerves were in the past, and I liked them there. The past was the past. Of course, Dad didn't give up.

"Okay, okay," I sighed. "Well, I woke up nauseous ... but you'll be happy to know, I forced myself to eat."

"Good ..."

"Not good, because I puked a tiny bit in my mouth at the end."

"Mr. B. must've loved that!"

"I did *not* tell him." Dad knew Mr. B. from all the years of helping with track and cross-country. One time, a kid vomited at the end of a race, and Mr. B. said, "You've run a good race, if you're puking at the finish line." Dad could relate, and thought Mr. B. was hilarious ever since.

"And I see you have your braids and lucky shorts," Dad said, with a smile.

"Of course. But *fresh* socks," I teased.

"Hey! I needed my lucky socks," Dad said, pointing his finger at me.

"Well, they could've been *clean* and lucky," I laughed.

"You sound like Nonna! Oh, she'd get so mad at me for hiding them, but I couldn't have her washing out the luck!"

"What did she say to you, again?"

"Say? More like shout!" Dad laughed. "She'd be so disgusted and yell, *'fa schifo!'*"

"*Fa schifo,*" I repeated, smiling at Dad. Nonna might've said the same thing if she saw his hair.

"And your playlist helped?" Dad asked.

"Yerp. Actually, I had a good song stuck in my head."

"One of my picks?"

"Maybe," I smiled, and decided to have some fun with him. "I hate to tell you ... I cut some more of your songs."

"Have some mercy ... I'm in the hospital!" he begged, and clutched his chest. The playlist Dad made for me in fifth grade was his idea of a magic potion for my nerves, and he didn't take it well when I made changes. Additions were fine, even Mom's disco was okay with him. He just couldn't handle his songs being deleted.

"You did *not* get rid of 'Born to Run'!"

"Dad! I *told you,* I like that one now. Guess again." I only felt a little mean, teasing him. He picked up his phone and started to scroll down his list.

"Hmm. No clue. Just tell me."

"'It Keeps You Running' ..." I said in the most mono-tone voice I could do.

"No! Why'd you dump that one?"

"Because it does *not* keep me running! It is sooo boring!"

"But it's steady ..."

"Boring." I cut him off and we laughed. Dad propped himself up and was still laughing, when he let out a chunky-sounding cough. He leaned to get a tissue, and then he spit into it.

"You want some water?" I asked, trying to not think about the gob in the Kleenex.

"Yeah, pass me that cup?" He took a sip and kept going.

"You can have your opinions, but try not to be so heartless about my music."

"Fine, fine. But really, Dad, the Doobie Brothers? Such a bad name."

"Hey, it's just a name ..." Dad started to say, just as Lucas charged in and threw himself across Dad's legs.

"Hey little man, get up here and give me a hug!" Dad laughed as Mom trailed in.

"Lucas, take it easy with Daddy! Josie, honey! Congratulations!" Mom said, as she kissed my head and ran a finger along my braid.

"How are you feeling today?" Mom asked Dad, putting her hand on his shoulder. Mom and Dad got along pretty well, for people who were divorced. I never even heard them fight. Still, somewhere between getting along and not fighting, were two people who didn't want to be married anymore. I didn't get it, but it worked.

"Better after watching Josie's race. And now seeing this guy!" He brushed back Lucas's hair and kissed him. "How was school today?"

"Good! We're writing speeches. Mine's a surprise, though, so don't ask," Lucas said.

"Aw, come on!" Dad smiled and gave him a squeeze.

"Nope. And don't try tickling it out of me."

"Like this?" Dad tickled Lucas and he squealed.

"I am not going to tell you, so stop!"

"Yes, sir!" Dad said.

"So—wait, someone taped your race?" Mom asked.

"Taped?" I asked.

"Okay. Eye-roll not necessary. Can I see the … what … recording?" Mom asked.

"Oh, I want to see, too!" Lucas wedged in next to Dad, and Mom and I crouched over to watch.

"That's awesome. Send it to me, will you? I want to watch it again later," Mom said.

"Okay, but don't go posting it." I had to lay down my terms. Mom was too much of a sharer.

"So, are we going for pizza to celebrate?" Lucas asked.

"No way! It's got to be sushi," I said as Lucas slumped. "Is that okay, Mom?"

Mom nodded. Sushi and Tea was our family go-to place for celebrations, like races or birthdays, but for Lucas, celebrating always meant pizza.

"Can we go for gelato after?" Lucas asked.

"Maybe, if we have time. It depends on how much homework you two have."

"Whaaaat?" My brother's arms flew up.

"Way to ruin a celebration, Mom," I said.

"Just eat as fast as you ran," Dad smiled.

CHAPTER 5

"MIDDLE DISTANCE RUNNER"

"I still think pizza would be way better! You always say you need carbs," Lucas said, giving it one more try.

"*Before* a race, Lucas," I said.

"But you do need them," he insisted.

"And protein and vegetables," Mom added in a chipper voice. Carbs and protein, *like breadsticks and prosciutto,* I thought. I had a week before Citys. A week till breadsticks and prosciutto meet again.

The smell of steamed rice and soy sauce greeted us when we got to Sushi and Tea. We slipped into my favourite booth, with the red kimono picture on the wall, and I gave us all chopsticks from the wooden box on the table.

Lucas pulled the chopsticks apart, scraped them together like he was sharpening them, and then played them like drumsticks, tapping along with the soft, chime music.

We placed our usual order of edamame, tempura, a variety of maki rolls, and Mom's sashimi. Mom was pouring us green tea, when I saw someone with distinctive grey hair passing our table.

"Oh, hey, it's Ms. Starter," I said.

"Who?" Lucas asked.

"Ms. Starter. The lady who starts the races," I said softly. She was talking to the guy making sushi behind the counter, when Mom turned to look. "Mom! Not so obvious!" I hung my head.

"She's the one that went to the Olympics," Mom said.

"What?" I straightened up to give Mom the stink eye. "She blows the horn at the start of races!" Mom always pulled things from thin air, and it was pretty exasperating.

"I know that. I haven't missed that many!" Mom replied. "Her name is Aurora something. She ran the ... oh, wait, I know it. Darn! I can't remember. One of those middle-distancey races like Dad used to run."

"What? When?" I asked, surprised that I didn't know or remember something like that, but Mom did. I was *not* surprised that Mom only had part of the information. Or that she made the middle-distance races of 800, 1500, and 3000 metres sound cutesy, when they were exhausting.

"I don't know. A while ago," she responded.

"I could've guessed that," I said, looking over and trying to picture Ms. Starter as an athlete. She was thin like an athlete, but that didn't mean anything. Mom was thin, too.

The server brought the edamame, and I put a salty pod into my mouth, sliding the beans out with my teeth. A meal had to have some green, according to Mom, and these were an easy sell. Lucas had a mouthful of edamame, when his eyes widened.

"She's leaving with take-out!" he said. Ms. Starter was heading our way toward the door. I tipped my face into my teacup.

"Hi, Ms. Starter!" Lucas said, his wave lifting him up out of his seat.

"Well, hello," Ms. Starter said, stopping next to our table. Her pastel-coloured blouse flowed behind her like a cape, so different from her track-meet neon. Mom introduced us, and Ms. Starter said her name was Aurora Osborne. Mom rambled something about it being such a great day for track, as if she'd been there. Mom didn't have a clue about boundaries, and saw nothing creepy about talking to total strangers—often in line for coffee, or at a store. My embarrassment was usually quick, but still painful. *No one will notice if I just slip under the table,* I thought.

"Josie won today," Lucas interrupted.

"Oh, congratulations," Aurora said, with a big smile that instantly gave me the warm fuzzies.

"Thanks," I smiled, fiddling with my chopsticks. A second earlier, I had wanted to hide, and then I hoped she'd recognize me.

"What race did you run?" Aurora asked. Nope. She definitely did not recognize me.

"I ... um, the 400."

"Seventh, eighth grade?" she asked. "Sorry, I'm not great at telling ages."

"Eighth."

"Oh, my goodness! That race was a fight to the finish! Great job!"

"Thanks." My cheeks warmed as I sat back in the booth.

"And did you run today, too?" she asked Lucas.

"No, I don't like running," Lucas said, making a face. "But I do parkour, and I swim and bike and ..."

"Okay, Lucas," I said, trying to shut him up.

"Sounds busy. Especially for you." Ms. Starter nodded at Mom, who agreed. "Ah, I think this is yours," she said, as the server came with the tray. "Have you eaten here before?"

"It's our favourite celebration place," Lucas said.

"Mine, too," she beamed and lifted the plastic bag in the air.

"Sorry to hold you up," Mom said.

"Oh, no, no. It was nice of you to say hello," she said, and waved as she headed out.

"Bye, Aurora!" Lucas said, over Mom and me. Not that I was very loud.

Lucas called out another goodbye, while I was still trying to process things. I met Ms. Starter! And if Mom was right about the Olympics thing, that made it even more special. I took the soy sauce from the tray, and tipped some into the little bowl.

"Well, how nice was she?" Mom asked, more like a statement.

"Very," I said with a mouthful of dragon roll.

"I thought you would've asked her about the Olympics," Mom said, as she dabbed some wasabi into her soy sauce.

"No way!" I said, shaking my head. I was thankful that Mom hadn't asked Ms. Starter a bunch of questions, either.

"I'm sure she's used to it. I purposely didn't ask her anything, in case you wanted to," she said.

"That would've been mortifying!"

"Well, she seemed like she would've been very open to talking."

"Not everyone is as big a sharer as you." I picked up another piece of sushi and dunked it into the soy sauce.

"Well, she sure was impressed with your race. That's pretty cool, honey," Mom smiled, and tapped her chopstick on her cup. I smiled as I chewed. The compliment from Ms. Starter felt great, not just because of how hard the race was, but because of how hard it was *before* the race. I was going to have to face Prosciutto again next week at Citys, plus there'd be more competition from the other divisions. I pushed away the feeling of having her alongside me.

"And you know what else is cool? We have the same favourite restaurant as someone who went to the Olympics," Lucas said, taking a piece of tempura.

"Coming from the boy who wanted pizza," I said, leaning into him.

CHAPTER 6

"INNER NINJA"

"We're going to be late!" Lucas yelled from the front hall.

"We're fine," I said as I walked downstairs, checking the bus app on my phone. I grabbed my lunch off the counter and stuffed it into my bag. Lucas was clipping his keychain onto his belt loop. I slid into my Birks and opened the door.

"Come on! I am *always* waiting for you!"

"What? Not funny!" Lucas bolted out the door and jumped from the top step, shouting, "Parkour!"

I locked the door and caught up to him tightrope-walking on our neighbour's stone ledge. Without hesitating or wobbling, he leapt onto a boulder and skipped along the rock garden, avoiding every plant.

Lucas wasn't what you'd call sporty, but when he'd started watching parkour videos, he got the bug. Mom found Mo's Monkey Obstacle and took Lucas once, but then Dad started taking him every weekend. The B.O. smell was too much for Mom to handle.

"I keep thinking a speech about superpowers would be better," Lucas said.

"Well, too late now," I said, unsympathetically.

"If I don't end up presenting today, though, I could rewrite it and do a superpower speech tomorrow."

"No. I think Scrabble being your favourite game is just so ... you. Are you nervous?"

"Naw. Should I be?" Lucas hopped off a low wall to walk beside me.

"No. I didn't think you would be. Just wondering. I would definitely not be as cool about it as you."

"Well, I could never race, so we're even."

Lucas was still talking to me about superpowers when we heard the familiar bellowing.

"It's Gigi!!" Lucas said, pointing and bolting up the street. I jogged behind him. We passed two apartment buildings, and I looked at the corner building across the street. The old woman we called Gigi, short for Granny

Greeter, was leaning out of her fifth-floor apartment, shouting at the world. Her windows were decorated with small flags from all over, and whenever we saw her, she'd be stuck out the window with the Canadian and U.S. flags above her head. She definitely wasn't speaking English, though, or even French.

"Shloyte! Reebatz! Flong-deepa!" she shouted to the people and cars below. Whatever it was, it sounded pretty darn urgent. We'd "known" Gigi for a few years, and it was funny watching people twirling around, trying to figure out where the sound was coming from. It was impressive how many blocks her voice carried.

When the light changed, we started crossing, and Lucas waved from the middle of the road.

"Hello!" he called up to her. She paused for a second, gave him the sweetest "Oh, hi!" and then went right back to her ranting.

"Getting Gigi to stop shouting is your real superpower," I laughed, as we got to the bus stop that was in front of her building.

"Ha! Yeah, maybe. I'm just glad she's okay," Lucas said.

"Seems completely fine ... and still a little angry."

"I was worried," he said.

"About what?"

"Her," he said, pointing up. "We haven't seen her in weeks."

"So, you were worried? We don't even know her," I said, leaning against the building by the bus stop. I really didn't get my brother's thinking sometimes.

"I mean ... I didn't worry all the time." Lucas stepped toward the curb and looked up at the building. "She's always in pyjamas."

"No wonder you like her so much," I smirked.

"I do. And even though we can't understand her, she still makes us smile."

"Oh, that she does," I said, just as she yelled something that sounded like, "Oonosh dunga!"

"I feel kind of bad that I forgot about her," I added.

"That's what I'm afraid of ... forgetting people that make me smile," he said as the bus pulled up.

"You're ten, and your memory is way better than mine. Stop with the worrying!" I said and stepped onto the bus.

Lucas had the chatty Mom gene, and often talked to people on public transit, some he knew and some he didn't know. All that reading on the Internet gave him endless "fun facts" to share. It was hard to keep up. Lucas once said it just made him happy to be sociable, and I joked that he'd talk to roadkill. He thought that was the grossest thing I ever could've said.

While Lucas was happily socializing on the bus, I went back to my phone, flipping through the pictures of Aurora that I'd looked up after we got home from dinner. Her legs had so many muscles, the kind I only saw on people in the Olympics. I found out she ran the 800-metre, so Mom was right about her being a "middle-distancey" runner. She looked so young, and when I zoomed in on her face, her expression was fierce. *She could've been the originator of lady balls.*

Lucas and I came out of the station. We wove through the rush hour crowd. Café doors pushed sweet smells of muffins and coffee toward us. A few blocks from school, Lucas stopped and put his forehead on the window of Sugar Mountain.

"Avert your eyes, Lucas."

"We should get Daddy that black licorice he likes, and bring it to the hospital."

"I doubt he'll be there long," I said, hoping there wouldn't be many more visits before he could go home.

"Dad said Nonna used to love that licorice, too. Do you think it's genetic?"

"Mmmm, no clue. I know she liked a black licorice drink. It was booze, but I remember her giving me a sip."

"I don't really remember her," he said, skirting around a guy pushing a stroller.

"You were too little. I mainly remember she liked feeding us. And she had 'bingo wings,'" I said, thinking back to sitting at her kitchen table when she cooked. She'd bring me a bowl of tomato sauce with a thick slice of bread to dunk, and when she'd set it down, I'd squish the flab of her arm. She'd pretend to be mad as she tickled me, and I just laughed and snuggled in. I should've called her a pillow person. *My* pillow person.

"I wish I remembered. And before you say it ... no, I do not want that to be my superpower."

"Remembering everything would be cool," I suggested.

"Flying or granting wishes are still top of my list," Lucas said, as my phone pinged in my bag.

"Text from Bird, she and Sofia are at Rasi's. Get moving those little legs!"

"Hey, I'm not the runner!" he said, as his backpack bounced up and down behind him.

We turned onto Erskine Street, passed the dry cleaners, and saw Bird and Sofia in front of Rasi's mini mart. Sofia dumped her sequined knapsack on the sidewalk and skipped over to us, pushing a roll of paper into my hand, while Bird stood there, eating a chocolate-covered ice cream bar.

"For you!" Sofia smiled, her face as cheery as her rainbow-striped top. I unrolled a "Congratulations – First Place" poster of a giant blue ribbon, complete with a JF Penguin and blue glitter.

"Aw, shmanks, Sofe. I'll hang it in my room." Sofia was always making pictures, cards, and things like that. She was more creative than I'd ever be.

"How's it going, Kookie Lukie?" Bird asked, as she took another bite, catching a piece of chocolate that was about to fall.

"Is that your breakfast?" Lucas asked, staring at the ice cream.

"More of a snack. A dee-lish, chocolaty, milk-ice snack! Want a bite?" Bird held it, and Lucas made a slurping sound.

"Thanks, Bird! Josie would never get this as a snack."

"She doesn't understand chocolate like we do, Kookie Lukie," Bird said, offering him another bite.

"You're way nicer than my sister."

"Don't you forget it," Bird said.

"Never!" Lucas smiled at me as he took another bite.

CHAPTER 7

"RACE TO THE BOTTOM"

Mr. B. was at his desk, with a bunch of kids laughing around him, when we walked into science class. I only saw his lemon-yellow shirt, but knew there would be brown pants and matching yellow shoes. He was always coordinated like that, and his shoes usually matched his shirts.

"It's the poo-pee outfit," Bird whispered to me.

"So mature," I replied.

"I happen to like those colours together. Outside a toilet," Sofia said in all seriousness. I figured she had Mr. B.'s outfits memorized and ranked by colour combinations.

"Do you think his girlfriend shops with him?" I asked.

"No way, he has his own sense of style," Sofia said.

"And she's way too cool to pick out some of his outfits," Bird added. We had only ever seen Mr. B.'s girlfriend in the photo on his desk and, once, when she picked him up in her orange mini. That car was all we needed to declare her *cool*.

"All right, everyone. How about you get in your groups, so I can take attendance, and you can get finished with these water filters."

"Yay!" Sofia clapped, leaning on our pushed-together desks.

"I think that's ten times," Bird said.

"Shush. This experiment is fun, and I get to be with you for a change," Sofia said.

"Yeah, Bird, she's finally in a good group," I said, smiling.

"And I'm going to get a good grade!" Sofia tapped the tips of her fingers together. Sofia always tried hard, but math and science were tough for her. Sometimes she had trouble organizing her thoughts, too, so writing essays didn't come easy, either. I told her it was because she had so many ideas trying to get out at once, and I really could see sparks flickering in her eyes when she would talk about things. I just hated when she felt dumb, because she was way smarter than me in a lot of ways.

I got our half-built tower from the shelf, and waited while Sofia and Bird gathered the rest of the materials: water bottle, funnels and coffee filters, sand, pebbles, charcoal-carbon stuff, popsicle sticks, and duct tape.

"Hey, how about we go for the no homework angle and try to finish up fast, and write the report in class," I suggested.

"Always thinking, Josie!" Sofia giggled.

"And all about being speedy since yesterday," Bird said as we laughed.

"Having fun?" Mr. B. asked. He gave a double-knock on our desk and kept moving. That guy didn't miss a thing.

"Hand me our beautiful duct tape," Bird said.

"You have to admit, pink and orange are happy colours," Sofia said. We checked our design and picked up where we'd left off, building our tower and adding the funnels.

"So, are you guys going to be able to sleep over Saturday after the fair?" Bird asked, taking a pile of popsicle sticks.

"Definitely," I said.

"Yes! Three more sleeps! I put it on our home calendar," Sofia said, handing us pieces of duct tape for the frame.

"So organized! And hey, my mom said she'd make us breaded chicken for dinner," Bird said.

"Oh, I love your mom," I said.

"I love your mom, too ... and her chicken," Sofia said.

"And Bird's brother," I teased as I taped sticks together.

"Stop!" Sofia said. She used to hide notes around Bird's older brother's room when we were younger. She'd put "Hi" or "Boo" in places like his shoes, which Bird thought was hilarious. Bird encouraged anything that might annoy her brother. Sofia had always denied any crush, and I was amazed at how she wasn't embarrassed in the least. She was bold and badass like that.

"Ooooh! And he said he would get us some booze," Bird whispered.

"What?" Sofia asked.

"Bird and I were talking about it yesterday. What do you think?" I asked, looking around for the bright yellow shirt, just in case Mr. B. was within earshot.

"What's he going to get us?" Sofia asked.

"Does it matter?" Bird laughed.

With our tower structure built, we added the "filters" to the funnels: pebbles in the top level, sand in the middle, and charcoal on the bottom. Underneath the tower was the last and main filter in the cut water bottle— a coffee filter, which I was supposed to add.

"Oh! I almost forgot!" Sofia said, grabbing her hoodie off the back of the chair, and taking a pink mesh ball out of her pocket. "The scrubby for the top!"

"Okay... go for it," I said. Sofia topped the tower with her pink scrubby.

"Voila! The icing on the pie!" she declared.

"Or cake?" Bird smirked.

"But I don't like cake," Sofia said. It made me think about Nonna's mixed-up sayings, not that I remembered them all, but Dad used to tell me. His favourite was when Nonna scolded him about "burning the bridge at both ends."

"Well, hey, the pink puffball does make a statement. Let's get Mr. B.," I said and called him over.

Mr. B. came to our desk, pinching his goatee. It's what he did when he was thinking hard.

"It's quite ... jazzy. I like the cotton-candy crown," Mr. B. said, poking at the pink scrubby.

"Cotton candy!" the three of us echoed. This was a food group we could all get behind.

"All right! Where'd this puffball come from?"

"Me!" Sofia said, raising her hand.

"Looks good, Knudsen. Though not for much longer. Let's get some of my special cocktail through this cotton candy tower and see how it filters." Other kids came around to watch. Sofia grabbed my hand and squeezed.

"Sofia! Nails digging in!" I said, turning to her. She released her grip but started to whimper, as Mr. B. poured muddy water onto the pristine pink scrubby.

Bird and I bent in close to see the water pass through each funnel; first pebbles, then sand, and carbon, seeming a little clearer each time. Just before the water dripped to the last filter, it was me who squeezed Sofia's hand.

"I forgot the coffee filter!" I said, as the pale, cloudy water filled the cup under the bottle.

"Oh, no," Bird said.

"Is that going to mess up our grade?" Sofia asked, her chin all bunched up.

"Not if we write an excellent report. Right?" Bird asked and Mr. B. nodded.

"I ... I'm really sorry, Sofia," I said, trying to think how I could make it up to her.

"It's okay," Sofia said.

"You're going to let her off that easily?" Bird asked.

"I have an idea," Mr. B. started, "Tomaselli takes a sip for the mistake."

"Eww, Mr. B.! You can't make her do that!" Sofia said.

"I'm just kidding, Knudsen," Mr. B. laughed.

"I still think she owes you. We'll figure something out, Sofe," Bird said.

"Yes!" Sofia laughed.

"Thanks a lot!" I said to both of them. And then I looked at Sofia and said *thank you* again, more quietly. I couldn't have wished for a better friend.

CHAPTER 8

"RUNNING UP THAT HILL"

Unfortunately, we didn't finish the water-filter report in class, so I did my section at home before going for a run. I still felt bad for letting Sofia down, but when I offered to help her, she insisted on doing it herself.

"Hi and bye," I said, as Mom came in the door. I tied my shoelace and stood up to go.

"What about homework?"

"Done."

"All of it?"

"Yerp. It wasn't much," I said, trying to get around her. She stepped aside, but only a smidge, because, of course, she wasn't finished telling me things. Always telling me things.

"You can always do a little extra, you know. Where are you going?"

"To the park."

"Okay. Be careful of traffic."

"So, I shouldn't run into the road?" I asked as I was leaving.

"That's enough sass!" Mom called from the doorway.

Mom admitted she said obvious things like "be careful," because it was part of the job of being a mom, and she couldn't help it. Most of Mom's bossiness, though, had to do with school. She actually had no real input when it came to running—the most she did was get me sports bras to "protect the girls." Even though there were really no girls to protect yet. The mini bomboloni on my chest did not bounce when I ran.

I hit shuffle on my playlist and "Middle Distance Runner" guided me toward the park, dodging people and strollers, past the stores and restaurants that lined the street. A cool breeze kept me from breaking a sweat, and after twelve minutes of running, my shadow led me into the park. I picked up the pace by the off-leash dog area, tennis courts, and playground, where kids were climbing, and darting through sprinklers shaped like giant flowers.

Training with Mr. B. at school was good, but nothing as killer as running the hill with Dad. I'd never run it by myself before. The path curved toward me at the bottom of the hill, and I glimpsed the eagle statue at the top. *Here I come,* I thought, as I tapped the timer on my watch and sped up.

I tilted forward as I started up the hill. I was pretty much on my toes when I stumbled. *Maybe this isn't such a good idea.* About halfway up, my legs were pretty pissed off at me. I pumped my arms, and thought back to when Dad and I ran up together. He wasn't one of those guys who'd let their kid win. Not at games, cards, and not any kind of race. Sometimes he'd have a cramp, or pretend to, and I'd get ahead of him, but then he'd be right on my heels, goading me. "I'm on you!!" he'd say. I fell into his trap, but gave it all I could, gasping and giggling. He still beat me most times. At the top, he'd flap his arms like an eagle and dance around in victory. And while I caught my breath, we'd look out toward downtown, Dad pointing to places, like where he worked or his new apartment, and then it was back down to do it again.

I imagined him spurring me on, as I pushed toward the eagle statue. I hit the timer at the top, fifty-two seconds. Not great. I rested my hand on the cold, pink granite base, under the bronze eagle that stood there with its wings outstretched, ready to take off. I searched for the landmarks Dad had showed me, but I was just procrastinating. *Go again,* I thought.

I was careful not to twist my ankle jogging down, and the next time up, I had competition from a dog, whose owner had chucked a ball for it to fetch. Dang dog was faster. After the third time up, I rested my head on the granite, feeling relief from the coolness, as I thought about Dad. He was such a joker, the way he made a big deal about winning. I mean, what kind of guy gets satisfaction from beating a little kid? We both knew he could beat me, but he was always so happy when I didn't give up. And there were a lot of times I didn't think I'd make it to the top, but I had to keep going. That was what mattered to him. That I kept on trying.

I was stretching my quads with one hand on the statue, when I heard a voice say, "Careful." I turned and saw Ms. Starter, chugging in slow motion toward me. I had noticed an old person jogging along the top of the hill, but with the hat and hair pulled back, I didn't recognize her.

"Oh, hi. Careful about what?" I asked.

"You have to watch out. There's a rumour that the eagle spits," she said, her big smile infectious.

"I never heard that," I chuckled.

"Oh, yeah, you've got to be careful. You're the 400 kid, right?"

"Yes. I'm Josie."

"Right. So, you're doing some hill training?"

"Yeah. I think I'm done, though."

"It's tough. No one runs up the hill for fun, do they?"

"Just the dogs," I said, pointing over at the dog that wasn't slowing down yet.

"True!" Ms. Starter laughed. "I do laps at the top here, where it's relatively flat."

"Makes sense. You don't want to fall."

"Ha! True. Already did that." She smiled and tapped her knee, reminding me of what I'd read. Her event was the 800-metre, where runners start in their own lanes, but then cut in after the first curve and run all packed together. She'd had a collision and a bad fall in an Olympic semi-final, but had got up and hobbled to the finish. She came last. And her knee was so messed up, she couldn't compete anymore.

"Oh, I'm sorry, I didn't mean to ... it's just ... I slipped on the hill ..." *Shut up, Josie.* I wanted the eagle to cover me with its wings. Or live up to the rumour and spit on me.

Ms. Starter laughed. The lines on her face were like a map of every trail she'd run.

"No apology necessary. It's one of many things that's shaped me. So, tell me, is your coach making you train on the hill?"

"No. I usually do it with my Dad, but today I just decided it might help for Citys."

"Oh, it will. Do you practise on a track at school, too?" she asked.

"There's a track at the high school next to my school."

"Well—listen, I can give you some drills to try, if you want. I help out at a running club, and it's something we give the kids to do," she said, as she rummaged around in her fanny pack and took out a pen. "I thought I had some paper ..."

"Is it much? You can write it on my hand," I said, reaching out.

"Okay. What times should I give you?" she asked, looking at the eagle. She nodded as if the eagle answered, and then wrote numbers on the top of my hand.

"It's pretty straightforward. You're going to run each distance, and try to hit those times exactly. Then you walk back to where you started, that'll be about a one-minute break in between, and then you'll do it again, maybe three or four times total. You got it?"

"So, like, I need to run 300 metres in 63 seconds? Exactly?" I asked, my face or my voice, or probably both, giving away my doubt.

"That's right! But it's not easy. You won't get it the first time, and maybe not the tenth, so don't get frustrated ... it's worth giving it a try. Like anything. Okay?"

"Sure! I'll try."

"Okay, I best keep moving."

"Wow, thank you, Ms ..."

"Aurora," she said.

"Thanks, Aurora," I said, smiling at my hand.

We said our goodbyes and headed in opposite directions. I was pooped jogging home, but got a boost thinking this might actually help me improve. I looked at the numbers.

$$300 = 63$$
$$800 = 2{:}48$$
$$400 = 1{:}24$$
$$200 = 42$$

Wait until I tell Dad.

CHAPTER 9

"*EVERYTHING NOW*"

I floated in the front door, still unable to believe Ms. Starter—Aurora—had given me running advice.

"Don't take your shoes off, we're going to see Dad," Mom said, as soon as she saw me.

"Oh, Mom! I'm sooo tired!"

"We won't go for long."

"I need a shower!" I said, thinking I'd better write the numbers down before I washed my hands.

"You're fine," she said, and leaned in for a sniff.

"Gross!" I said, dodging away from her.

"I have to help Sofia with homework," I added, thinking that would get me out of having to go.

"And Lucas has his speech to work on, and I have a report to finish, too. We'll be back in plenty of time," Mom said.

"What about dinner?" Lucas asked.

"We'll grab BLTs and eat with Dad."

"Oh, yay!" Lucas sat on the floor and slid his shoes on.

"Can't just you and Lucas go?" I did want to tell Dad about Aurora, but sending a text to him would do. Mom grabbed her keys from the table.

"No. The longer you whine, the more time you waste. Let's go."

■

Mom was annoying. Going to the hospital was annoying. Being so annoyed was getting annoying. I knew not to argue. I wanted to chill more than I wanted to see Dad, and I knew that made me a self-centred, horrible person.

Dad was asleep when we got to his room, so Mom went downstairs to get food. His mouth gaped open, and his breath gurgled in and out. I was trying to find the TV remote, while Lucas tiptoed over to the side of the bed. Dad woke up suddenly and grabbed Lucas's arm.

"Aah!" Lucas jumped.

"Ha! Hey, champ! Did I scare you?" Dad pulled Lucas in next to him and kissed his head.

"Nooo. But your snoring was pretty scary!"

"Scary? Like this? That's what I call scary!" Dad said, tussling Lucas's mop of hair. Then Dad looked at me.

"And how's my speed-demon?"

"Good," I said, giving him a kiss. His hair was clean. "Guess what?"

"What?"

"You know the old lady who starts all our races? The one who was in the Olympics?"

"Yeah, Aurora ... um ... Aurora Osborne."

"We met her!" Lucas jumped in.

"Wow," Dad said.

"Yeah, she was getting sushi last night and then ..." I started.

"Josie was scared to say hi to her, so I did," Lucas said. He sounded proud of himself, but really, talking to strangers was nothing new for him.

"Yeah, well, anyway, *today* I ran to the park and up the hill, and she was there, running! By the eagle!" I didn't want Lucas to sabotage my story.

"Wow. She's still running ... awesome," Dad said.

"Well, more like shuffling!" I laughed.

"What is this?" Lucas said, leaning back on Dad, and taking a card off his bedside table.

"It's a prayer card that a friend of Nonna's brought for me today," Dad said.

"*As I was saying* ... Ms. Starter, I mean, my new friend Aurora ... Ha! Well, we got talking, and she gave me these drills to help me train. She said they do it at her running club." I held out my hand to Dad, and watched as he ran his finger along the numbers.

$$300 = 63$$
$$800 = 2{:}48$$
$$400 = 1{:}24$$
$$200 = 42$$

"This is very cool, sweetheart."

"You know how it works?"

"Sure. I bet it'll help with your pace."

"She said it could get frustrating." I sat in the chair and tapped on the numbers with one finger. "I don't know. What if I can't run 200 metres in 42 seconds, or 300 in exactly 63 seconds, or any of it? I only have five days to try."

"It's not easy, but you'll get it." Dad smiled at me. It was the look he always had when I didn't think I could do something. It was the look that told me I could do it. I believed that look. A mirror never gave me a look as believable.

"So, is this saint named after a peregrine falcon?" Lucas asked, waving the card at Dad.

"I don't think so, Lucas. But maybe." Dad laughed.

"Says he's a 'Wonder Worker.' Do you think saints have superpowers?" Lucas bounced on the bed.

"Some people probably think so," Dad said. "I know Nonna did, and that's why her friend gave it to me." I took the card from Lucas.

"Hey!" he protested. There were words on one side, and a picture of a guy in a long black robe, holding a long stick like a shepherd, with his bloody leg sticking out.

"Yuck." I set the card back on Dad's side table, hoping Lucas wasn't going to ask more about this Peregrine person. I guessed Dad was done, too, because he slid the remote out from under his pillow and handed it to Lucas.

"Why don't you see what's on that retro channel," Dad said.

"Okay!" Lucas hopped off the bed and pointed the remote at the TV on the wall.

"Josie, what do you think about joining a running club, when you start high school in September?"

"Really? That'd be cool. Doing drills like this would be so different than just running laps, like Mr. B. has us do," I said.

"Well, he's been a good coach to you, but I think you're ready to take it up a notch. If you want," Dad said through a yawn. He tipped his head back on the pillow. I really liked the idea, but I didn't want Dad to think I'd ditch him for a fancy running club.

"We'd still run, too, right?"

"You might get too fast for me." Dad smiled as his eyelids drooped.

We watched *Gilligan's Island* for a little while, until Mom came in.

"Hello, hello!" she said, as she plopped a bag on the rolling table near the bottom of the bed.

"Well, hi there." Dad woke and smiled at her.

"Sorry it took so long ... the line was awful! Who's hungry?"

Lucas hopped off the bed, like a puppy going for a treat. Mom complimented Dad on how good he looked, while she unwrapped the food.

"Whoa, whoa ..." Dad started. "That bacon. You gotta get it out of here!" Dad coughed and spit into a tissue that he put on a pile. *So gross,* I thought.

"Why?" Lucas asked.

"It's all right," Mom said calmly. She wrapped the sandwiches back up and told Lucas to take them to the seating area down the hall.

"Hand me that dish!" Dad said, pointing next to me. I practically threw the curved blue bowl at him and backed away. I was not about to watch.

"Food out! *Now!*" Dad groaned. He dry-heaved into the bowl.

"Josie, it's fine. Go have your BLT with Lucas."

"Oh. That bacon smell is awful." Dad leaned back and closed his eyes. His forehead was all shiny.

"You love bacon. What's with all the drama?" I asked.

"Josie ...!" Mom gasped. Then she muttered, "How about using your filter?"

"What? Am I right, Dad? You're acting like it's going to kill you."

Dad opened his eyes a slit and curled his lip into a smile. Then he chuckled.

"Killed by bacon."

CHAPTER 10

"TROUBLE"

Silence in the car was a rarity. And I didn't just mean because of Lucas. Rides without him were like being held captive, while Mom talked, or forced me to talk. That meant silence on the way home from the hospital was a treat in one way, but I could tell it wasn't supposed to be.

We stopped at Chanatry's Market on the way home. Mom mumbled something as she flung the keys into her bag and opened the door.

"What?" I asked.

"Getting coffee and filters. You remember how to use your filter?" Mom asked and slammed the door.

"Whoa!" Lucas said. "Why's she mad about coffee filters?"

"She's not," I said, and shifted toward the window.

"Well, seems like it," he said. I didn't feel like getting into it. I'd had enough filters for one day. Besides the ones Mom went to buy, there was the one I forgot in science, and now, the filter that didn't work in me.

Mom was back pretty quickly, and as she started the car, Lucas dove right in.

"How come you're so mad about coffee filters?" Mom flung the car into a parking spot near the exit and turned the engine off. *Oh, crap.*

"A different kind of filter, Lucas. The filter I mean is what you use to keep a thought in your head, and not blurt it out of your mouth. For a ten-year-old, you have a pretty good filter."

"Oh. Thanks, Mom," he said.

She swiveled to face me. "You, on the other hand ... Josie, what the *hell* was that at the hospital?"

"Language, Mom!" Lucas scolded.

"Lucas, please. Josie, don't you see how insensitive that was?"

"I was being funny! Dad laughed!" I shrugged and put my hands up.

"Laughed at what?" Lucas asked.

"He did laugh ... but it doesn't make it okay," Mom said.

"My gosh, it just slipped out! Why are you making such a big deal out of it?" I asked. Lucas had unclipped his seatbelt and was leaning forward between the seats.

"I don't get why you're fighting," he said.

"Lucas, do you mind?" I snapped.

"Josie made a joke that I don't think was very funny," said Mom.

"Ugh." I turned to the window, my eyes rolling so far back, I couldn't see.

"Josie, look at me. I'd like you to stop and think a little," she said, pushing her hair behind her ear.

"I *do!*" I shouted.

"All right," Mom sighed. "I just thought it was a little insensitive."

"Well, Daddy didn't. Obviously, he has a better sense of humour than you."

"Obviously," Mom said as she started the car. "Lucas, honey, buckle up."

"I've got a good sense of humour, too," Lucas said.

"You're the funniest in the family, Lucas," I said, flatly.

■

When we got home, I was happy to hibernate in my room. I texted Bird and Sofia about Aurora, though it was still so weird to call her that. I couldn't shake the hospital scene, so I texted Bird about my bacon joke, partly to have her on my side.

Bird: You said that?

Me: lol

Bird: Even I think that's in bad taste

Me: Barfing over bacon?

Bird: Not exactly. But you are gross

Me: And you love me

Bird: Yerp

Me: ☺

"Can I come in?" Mom asked, as she came into my room.

"You're already in." I checked my phone, in case Bird had texted more. I didn't understand her answer to my bacon crack. Why didn't she think it was as funny as I thought she would?

"Wow. This room looks good," Mom said, patting a folded pile of clothes on my dresser. Then she sat down on my bed. It groaned, as if it expected a prolonged chat.

"Listen, I've been thinking, and I didn't want to get into all of this before ..." Mom slid her hands under her thighs. "Do you remember when Daddy first got sick a few years ago?"

"Yeah." I hugged Mr. Puffy and leaned against my headboard.

"I mean, after the operation."

"Yeah. Kind of."

"Remember how different your dad was. He was dealing with so much."

"Why do you bring up old stuff?" I asked, tipping my face into Mr. Puffy. When Dad found out he had cancer the first time, he had been awful. Short-tempered. Mean. Totally unlike the Dad I knew.

"To remind you to be more sensitive."

"I will be more sensitive," I said, mimicking her tone. Mom shook her head.

"I was also going to say that you are more mature now than two years ago—but maybe not so much."

"Sorry. It's not like before, though."

"No ... you're right," Mom touched Puffy's foot for a second and continued, "This isn't like last time. And he's concerned they haven't figured it out yet."

"What do you mean?"

"Mom! Mom!" Lucas yelled, barrelling up the stairs.

"In Josie's room," Mom called to him.

"I made a mistake and need more paper for my speech."

"There's some in my bottom desk drawer," Mom said. Lucas wagged his finger back and forth between Mom and me.

"Are you fighting again?" he asked. Mom told him we were just talking, and that she'd be down in a minute. I crossed my eyes and stuck my tongue out, just before he left.

"You know, I'd love to just praise you all the time, but when you've done something, or *haven't* done something, I can't just ignore it. I have to tell you."

"Okay, Mom. I get it. I'll be sensitive. You told me."

"Hah. You've been saying that to me since you were three," Mom said. Then we both smiled, and she said, *"You talk to me, too, too much."*

"Okay," I chuckled. "Are we done now?"

"Unless you have anything else you want to talk about? Oh! Like your new training regime?" Mom smiled.

"Hah! See, you are funny." I giggled at Mom's attempt to talk about running.

"No, I know you get your sense of humour from Daddy. Uh ... one more thing," Mom said, and I cringed. "Why aren't there any clothes on your floor?"

"Obviously, because I am mature."

CHAPTER 11

"11:11"

Hot, twitchy feet kept me awake. I kicked one foot out, both feet out, one back under, but could not cool them off. When this had happened in the past, Dad said it was because my feet would rather run than sleep. He suggested closing my eyes and thinking about running a circuit, and in no time, I'd be dozing. Some people counted sheep; I did laps.

I tried to imagine running the route around the school, but I couldn't shake what Mom had said about Dad. *This isn't like last time.* That should've been good. I thought back to all the things that started when I was ten: my parents split up, Daddy got sick, had a chunk taken out of his lung in a major operation, chemo, baldness, then he got better. Life was pretty normal the past two years. So, what was it they couldn't figure out this time?

There was an episode, just before Dad's operation, that I hadn't thought about in a while, until tonight, when Mom came into my room. Dad had been flying off the handle over all kinds of small things: not picking up stuff or closing a cereal box. *The jam incident,* though, was the worst.

It was a Saturday morning at Dad's house that started with the usual cartoons—

Lucas in a TV daze, and Dad in his leather chair, drinking coffee.

"Dad, can I make toast and have it in here?" I asked.

"Sure, just don't get anything on the couch."

"I won't."

I made the toast, brought my plate and the jam jar into the living room, and set everything on the coffee table. I kneeled on the floor, and started putting jam on my toast. It was such a treat to eat in front of the TV, like getting room service or something. By the second or third knife-full, some jam plopped on the table.

"What did I tell you?" Dad's voice boomed.

"Oh, sorry, I'll clean it." I got up and started walking

to the kitchen, wishing I'd been more careful.

"Hurry," he called, and I picked up the pace. "And make sure to squeeze the sponge out."

I came back in with the sponge and bent down.

"I told you to be careful," Dad snapped.

"I know. Sorry," I said, just as I accidentally smeared the jam on the table. The glob was bigger than I thought, and as I went to wipe it again, Dad's hand swooped in and *whack!* He hit my hand so hard, the sponge flew across the room, and my hand smacked the table. Stunned, I held my hand and cried. When I looked at Lucas, he was hugging his legs.

"What are you doing?" Dad shouted over me. His face came close; his expression was as sour as his breath. "That water will ruin the wood!"

"I'm sorry," I cried. He picked up the sponge and wiped. "Stop crying, and go get a towel to dry this up!"

Lucas was still frozen on the couch, when I ran back in with a towel. I stared at my pink hand as I wiped, holding in tears. It still stung. I couldn't believe this was all over a little blob of jam. It wasn't like I'd stained the couch. Dad handed me the sponge, and I brought that and the towel into the kitchen, scared and angry at the same time.

I pretty much hated Dad after that incident. I wasn't just a little miffed, like when he or Mom wouldn't let me do something. I was mad at his lashing out all the time, and whacking my hand over a little jam. I didn't want to see him, and when I told Mom why, she gave me the "he has a lot on his mind" explanation. It felt like more than that. He'd changed. He didn't act like the Dad that loved me. He never even apologized, and I wasn't ready to forgive him, even if he did.

The jam incident happened just before Christmas. Normally, the only time we went to church, after Mom and Dad got divorced, was on the weekends we were with Dad, but for some reason, Mom brought us to church on Christmas Eve. She definitely wasn't religious, but she liked the songs and decorations.

The church was modern and didn't feel like a church, though the huge crucifix was a dead giveaway. As the organ played, I looked at the expanse of stained-glass windows that fanned out from the altar. It was like an abstract collage of people, kneeling and facing the humongous cross. All the people in the church were doing the same, like they had conviction. They believed in something so clearly. They had faith. At that time, I was very confused about my feelings for Dad, and I wasn't sure what to believe.

Why had Dad gotten so mad? The way Dad acted had made it seem like he didn't love me anymore. It hurt, and I hated him for that. And I couldn't understand how I went from loving him so much to hating him. So, as I sat there in the church, and the Christmas song played, I made a wish. The eleven-year-old kind. I wished that if I still really loved Dad deep down, that he would get better and back to normal, and obviously, my love for him would be back to normal, too. But if I really hated him, like really, really, deep down hated him, then I wished he would just die.

It was a twisted wish, but it turned out all right. Dad got healthier and stronger, and my warm, fun Dad was back. And I loved him, of course. I didn't think about if it was magic or God, or anything, that made it happen. I just knew we were back to normal.

As I lay in bed, my feet no longer twitchy, I felt relieved that it was the good wish that came true. I wondered what came first, me realizing I loved Dad and he got better, or he got better and was lovable again. I understood how he was really afraid when he got cancer, and it took over.

Like Mom said. But being in the hospital again, he wasn't mean, or mad all the time. He didn't seem scared; he just got a little sick over a bacon smell, and *laughed* at what I said. It didn't seem the same as before. And even though he was back in the hospital, Dad was still fun and happy. The bacon thing must have been a blip, like a stomach ache. It had to be.

CHAPTER 12

"HALO"

On the bus ride to school, Lucas ran into a few friends and jumped right into video-game lingo. They spoke an unknown language, like Granny Greeter, when they used words like "mana," but even when they said regular words like "health" or "level," I still had no idea what they were talking about.

"Josie! You think Mom is going to make us go to church on Sunday?" Lucas asked. I looked up and saw we were passing by St. John's Church. Lucas was like a puppy, playing with one thing, and easily distracted by something else.

"I hope not," I said.

"Okay," he said, and plunged back into the video vortex with his buddies.

The idea of having to go to church, now that Dad was back in the hospital, hadn't really occurred to me. When Dad had his operation, Mom made us go to church while he recovered. She didn't come; she sent us. Something about her having "issues" with the Catholic Church. So, I figured we didn't really need to go, either, and I talked Lucas into going to the park instead. It was way more fun to lie on the spinning roundabout, looking at the sky, and listening to the hymn of Lucas's belly laugh. Seemed like a pretty holy hour to me, if you got around that we'd lied to Mom.

Lucas stayed with his video-game buddies from the bus station to school, but he caught up to me in the schoolyard.

"Can I have a good luck kiss?" he asked.

"For what?"

"My speech. Remember, I didn't do it yesterday? So, today's the day."

"Oh, right," I said, leaning down to kiss his cheek quickly. I really wasn't that embarrassed to kiss him, but just didn't want to make it a big deal. "Don't be nervous. It's about something you really like, and that comes through super clearly," I added.

"Yeah, I feel okay about it. I just figured the lucky kiss thing works for you."

"Ha. Sometimes." I thought about how I hadn't gotten a kiss from Dad before my last race.

"I'd like to get to the top five in my class, but it'll be okay if I don't."

"Think positive. And remember to pause at the funny parts."

"Oh, yeah. Like when I tell them the inventor's name is Alfred M. Butts!" Lucas chuckled.

"They'll *crack* up! Ha! Get it?" I clapped my hands, so proud of my joke.

"Ha! I get it!" he laughed.

"You'll do great."

"Thanks. Can I ask you another thing?" he said. I really hoped he wasn't going to ask me about going to church again.

"Sure."

"Do I have B.O.?" he asked. I was relieved, and so, without thinking, I leaned in and sniffed.

"Not at all, why?"

"Because I could smell something all the way to school, and I thought it might be me."

"It must've been one of your stinky friends. Maybe they just haven't washed in a while."

"Yeah, I don't smell it now. I tried smelling myself before, but I couldn't really reach my pit without being obvious."

"Well, it's not you. I thought you were going to ask me about church again."

"Yeah, I don't know why I asked about that. I guess it's just because Dad is in the hospital."

"Well, it's not like before with Dad, and I don't even think church is on Mom's radar. So don't go bringing it up."

"Okay, I won't," he said, as we started walking across the yard.

"And as for being stinky, you're the king of showers, plus you're still kind of young," I pointed out.

"I am coming of age, though," he said seriously, then whispered, "I'm even getting dilly hairs."

"Oh, please!" I burst out laughing and took a few steps back, like I was going to fall over. "You are not."

"I am, you meanie-bo-beanie. They're light, but even Mom saw."

"Like your moustache?" I laughed.

"Yeah," he said, as if the microscopic hairs above his lip were obvious.

"I rest my case," I said, but saw the hurt in his scowl. "Hey, the good news is, you don't have B.O., so you don't have to worry when you do your speech.

"I do actually feel pretty good about it," he said, as the bell rang, and we headed toward the doors.

"It's a good speech," I said.

"And the part about always beating you and Mom is pretty funny, too."

"Hilarious," I said.

CHAPTER 13

"FEEL GOOD INC."

Classes flew by, and I tried to find Lucas to remind him I had track practice, but figured he'd reconnected with his gamer posse and was heading home. Since our school didn't have a track, our practices were a block away at the high school. Bird and Sofia were waiting outside while I changed. They wanted to escort me, as if they were doing me a favour. We all knew it was really to check out the high school boys' rugby practice.

When I got outside, I heard screams from where Bird and Sofia were standing with a bunch of other people. I could just make out Bird stepping forward over her clasped hands, and without letting go, bringing her hands behind her butt, up around her back, her shoulders twisting so her arms could go over her head and back in front of her. It was her party trick that never got old.

"Do it again, Bird!" someone said as I got closer.

"Got to rest the shoulders ... and get her to practice," Bird said, as she picked up her knapsack. Sofia skipped next to us on the worn, dirt path that was a short-cut to the high school.

"Do I have a dumb laugh?" Sofia asked.

"What?" I said.

"Where'd you get that?" Bird asked.

"You didn't hear? Those guys called me 'Donkey' when I laughed."

"They're clueless. Don't listen to them," I said.

"Do *you* think I sound like a donkey when I laugh?" she asked.

"No!" Bird and I said together.

"Seriously, Sofe. Those guys are always making fun of something," Bird said, taking Sofia's hand.

"Maybe I need a nickname before *Donkey* sticks. A good one, like you and Bird have."

"My brother was three and couldn't say my name," Bird laughed.

"I don't have a nickname," I said.

"Yes. Speedy, or Leggy ..."

"No one calls me that," I said.

"I do," Sofia said, sliding her arm through mine.

"Aw, shmanks, Sofe."

"Maybe I just need to work on a new laugh, then," she said.

"No, you don't," I said, and Bird agreed. Sofia looked like she should've had the type of laugh that summoned fairies and bunnies. The sound she actually made was more like what you'd hear from a big, boisterous aunt with a moustache. Even when she was little, her laugh was like a horn. It was a big laugh to match her heart, and was probably what drew me to her. I thought I'd change the subject by pointing toward the rugby players on the field, but Sofia wasn't done. There were layers to this.

"Do I even look like I'm smiling when I laugh? I've checked myself out in the mirror and I look like I'm in pain."

"No, you don't ... you're smiling," I said, but I didn't think it registered with her.

"And sometimes, I think I am laughing, but ... I'm not! There's no sound at all. I'm just clapping. Like a seal. Har. Har. I'm surprised no one's thrown me a fish!"

"You'd never catch a fish," Bird said and I smiled.

"No, really! I'm serious. You guys have normal laughs. I've tried, but I can't do anything to change it."

"Why is this really a thing?" Bird asked.

"Yeah, we don't want you to change it," I said.

"So, you don't think I need to?"

"Nope."

"Never."

"And do you think I'm being stupid?"

"Nope," I said.

"Maybe a little," Bird smirked. "But only stupid in thinking you need to change, because some jerks called you *Donkey*."

"Exactly," I said, nodding toward Bird.

"Yeah, it's not a hee-haw at all. I actually think it's a little more like honking," Sofia said.

When we talked, it was easy. It was safe. We'd known each other for so long, we were okay to let our crazy thoughts and flaws fly. Like geese. Honking geese.

"Hey, Sofe, I know what will make you really smile," I said.

"What?" she asked, wiggling with excitement.

"Guess!"

"Nooo, just tell me?" Sofia stopped and slumped her shoulders forward, like she did when she was disappointed, or something stopped being fun.

"In the spirit of how I owe you for messing up our experiment, I thought maybe you could do my makeup for the fair Saturday night. And by makeup, I really just mean mascara. How's that?" I asked. Sofia jumped and twirled and chanted, "Yes!" over and over.

"I think she's happy," Bird smirked.

"You'll like it, Josie. You'll see. I promise, not too much."

"I trust you," I said.

"Oh, with your dark hair, it's going to look so good. This is going to be so fun!" Sofia said.

"Yeah, and I'm finally going to the fair at night!" I said.

"I know I'm not good at many things, but mascara will look so good!" Sofia said.

Bird clasped Sofia's shoulders as we neared the track.

"Sofe, Sofe, Sofia ... look at me." Bird's face was an inch from Sofia's. "Enough knocking! You're good at a lot of things. You've got to be kinder to yourself!" Bird tried to stay serious, but all three of us burst out laughing—with Sofia in full honk mode.

"I know!! Har-Har-Har! See? I mean, you hear me?"

Sofia clapped as she sucked in air.

"You did three honks that time!" I said.

"Oh my God!!" Bird laughed and almost fell to the ground.

■

We staggered up the bleachers and plopped our stuff down. The laughter was the perfect switch of gears for Sofia. She and Bird leaned into each other and looked onto the field, playing "I spy" about guys, while I got my running shoes out of my bag. I just listened to *who* thought *who* was *hot, hotter, and hottest,* while I tied my laces. Then I grabbed my water bottle, stood up, and took a sip.

"You two have fun playing your very interesting game."

"Better than running around in circles," Bird said.

"Yeah, right," I said, and ran down the steps, their cackles and honks pushing me to the track.

CHAPTER 14

"CIRCLES"

If running track was just mindlessly going around in circles, my friends were right about it being crazy. To them, I probably looked like a hamster on one of those wheels. And when I first started running track, I was like that; I'd run full steam until I was pooped, and then just drag the rest of the way. Dad taught me where to push, where to settle, and so I got better, but I really didn't know how to pace myself. Aurora's numbers were supposed to help me with that.

City Finals was in five days, but we never had practices on Fridays or over the weekend, so I knew this would be the last school practice. Mr. B. was a dedicated coach, but with a team of kids in Grades 4 to 8, with different abilities, he wasn't all that hardcore. Even though less than twenty of us made it to City Finals, his rah-rah spirit was pretty strong. He wore his penguin T-shirt and hat, with orange shorts and running shoes that perfectly matched the colour of the penguin's beak. He definitely made us feel we were a team, and we rooted for and consoled each other.

One of the twins who'd recorded my race waved to me as I got to the track. They were the only guys in eighth grade who qualified for City Finals, and being twins, I really had no idea who did hurdles and who did shot put.

"All right, athletes," Mr. B. said, clapping his hands. "So, we keep clear of the rugby practice; we're going to the diamond route to warm up!" Everyone groaned.

"I *love* your enthusiasm. So, listen up! To recap ... you go behind the baseball diamond, up the slope, run across the top along the fence, down the slope over there, back around the track this way, and repeat. Quit your whining. It's only for ten minutes."

I tapped my fingers on my hips, while the protests and moans continued. I looked at my hand with the numbers, anxious to get at it.

"I. Am. Not. Finished. Run at tempo. For you nonrunners, this means *comfortably* hard. Then meet me over by the stumpy pole, and I'll assign your individual drills." He waved his hand. "Gentlemen in the back, you got me? Nodding? That's good. All righty, move it out!"

After running to the eagle, going up and down the tiny slope was nothing. The twins joined me, and we ran together, and by the end of the warmup, it was easy to tell them apart. Hurdler-twin was quiet and ran with ease, occasionally hopping over an imaginary barrier. Shot-put-twin talked for both of them, and panted the whole time. I'd never thought about strategies for throwing, but I was fully informed during the ten-minute warmup. Shot-put-twin was so into it, he was already planning on doing javelin next year in high school, and both of them wanted to join a track club. They seemed as serious about track as I was, but I didn't feel like telling them that I was interested in joining a club, too.

When Mr. B. was finishing up with the younger kids, I went over to talk to him.

"So, Mr. B., would it be okay to try out this new training thing?" I said, showing him my hand. He held my fingers and looked.

"These times from your dad?" Mr. B. asked.

"No. You know Ms. Starter who starts all the races?"

"Yeah, of course."

"Well, I met her, and she gave them to me to try."

"Wow, Tomaselli! Well, we have to listen to an Olympian! Go for it, kid!"

"Thanks, Mr. B.," I said.

"Maybe keep it to the outside lane, so you have room."

"Already thought of that."

"Maybe take a break in between."

"Ms. Starter told me that, too."

"See? I'm such a great coach. Don't forget me when you go to the Olympics!"

"Oh, right, Mr. B." I laughed and looked at my hand.

$$300 = 63$$
$$800 = 2{:}48$$
$$400 = 1{:}24$$
$$200 = 42$$

■

I had never run 300 metres, so it seemed a little weird. I decided to walk around the track 100 metres, so three hundred metres would have me still end at the finish line.

I crouched down, left leg bent, hit my timer, and charged. I started hard, as if it was a race along the straight part of the track, took the curve and pushed the last hundred to the finish. I hit the timer as I crossed the line and slowed. Sixty-eight seconds. I thought I was going pretty fast but, obviously, I ran too slowly. Finding that pace, and adjusting it, wasn't going to be as easy. I walked back to the start, and waited a minute before running again.

The second time was faster, but not enough. I decided to try the 800. I had no idea how to go about this one, so I took it fairly hard the first lap, but I was so tired and slowed down the second time around. Obviously, I was way over the 2:48 time. I couldn't imagine Aurora doing this race with other runners packed all around, which gave me one more reason to dislike the 800m. No, thank you. *I'll stay in the 400m, in my own lane.*

Mr. B. came to check on me.

"How's it going, Tomaselli?"

"Terrible! It's so hard to hit these times."

"Well, you're not used to it. Good for you for trying. You do the 400 yet?"

I shook my head.

"So, skip the 800 and do the 400 next," he said. *As if*

I'm doing the 800 again, I thought.

I ran the 400-metre but was way slow. I was getting tired, as I walked to the start in the outside lane, remembering what Aurora had said about getting frustrated. I just wanted to hit one of these darn times. I bent down to start. *Come on, do this.* I pushed it a bit more at the start, and then again around the last curve to the finish. I checked my watch. I made it in 1:22, a few seconds too fast, but pretty close. Feeling some sense of accomplishment, I moved onto the 200-metre. The shorter distance was easier, even though I didn't get those times right, either.

Mr. B. called us in to do some strengthening exercises: donkey kicks, clams, lunges, squats, push-ups, and planks. For me, the cool-down stretches were the reward after the running. Mr. B. always did the exercises with us and, despite his belly, the guy was *unbelievably* limber. My favourite stretch was when he made us sit with our legs in a V and "reach, reach, reach, forward." I had to watch him go first. His legs were practically at 180, his belly squished flat, and his face nearly touched the ground. It was stunning—as in, astonishing, not beautiful. When someone once asked how he could do that, he said with a totally straight face, "My sister used to stand on my back."

CHAPTER 15

"GET WHAT YOU GIVE"

The aroma wafted up my nostrils when I came in the front door. Lucas was doing homework at the dining table, but by the time I dumped my knapsack and took my running shoes off, he was right in front of me.

"Guess what? Guess what? I made the top five!"

"Nice!" I said, holding up my hand for a high-five. Lucas jumped and squealed as he slapped my hand.

"What's cooking?" I asked him, as I headed to the kitchen.

"Mom's making Coney," Lucas said, and sat back down.

"Smells good, Mom," I said. Mom covered the pan with a clang.

"No inspecting." She held her arm out as a barrier. "Coney" dinner was the first and only thing Mom ever taught me how to cook. Named after a friend of hers, it was ground chicken, onions, black beans, corn, garlic, and soy sauce—all over rice. Quick and easy. The thing was, Mom always chopped onions really badly, and they ended up as a slimy pile of worms on the side of my plate. Cutting the onions into perfect, tiny pieces was usually my job.

I set my phone and ear buds on the counter and got a glass of water.

"How was practice?"

"Good. Hard."

"Did you work on that number thingy?" She gestured toward the faded numbers on my hand.

"Yeah. That's what was hard."

"Well, you're probably hungry—go wash up. Lucas, clear your stuff off the table," Mom said.

I peeked around the wall, put my hands to my chest like claws, and did my loudest baby velociraptor squawk.

"*Stop!!*" Lucas threw an eraser at me.

"Hah, how do you like it?" I teased.

"Hey! Enough. Go wash up!" Mom said.

After we washed our hands, Mom handed Lucas the

salad bowl and cutlery to bring to the table, and I got us all water. Mom piled a few scoops onto our plates, and carried them to the table like a professional server, a plate in each hand, one on her forearm. A talent from her restaurant days. Mom set the plates down. Moment of truth. I flattened the mound, ready to pick out onions.

"No onion?" I asked.

"There's onion," Mom said, in a way I wasn't so sure about. I took a bite, then raked through the meat and beans.

"Where?"

"Just look." Mom smiled.

"They're so small!" I said, as I tapped the plate with my fork. "Good job, Mom!"

"I'm glad I'm sitting. A compliment from the expert."

"It's always good to me," Lucas said, shovelling in a huge mouthful.

"Mom already likes you, so you don't need to suck up to her."

"I'm not," he said.

"Uh-huh."

"So ... Lucas, what was your best and worst today?" Mom asked.

"Best has to be, I'm in the top five for my speech."

Lucas wiggled in his seat. "And worst is, I don't know who to vote for."

"You vote for yourself!" I nudged his arm and knocked food off his fork.

"I can't do that," Lucas said, taking another scoop.

"Why not?" Mom asked.

"Feels kind of braggy."

"I can understand that, but if you think, out of the five speeches, that yours is the best one to represent your class, it's okay to vote for yourself. If you liked someone else's better, then you vote for them," Mom said.

"Don't you think someone running for president or prime minister votes for themselves?" I asked, and Lucas nodded.

"But ... I'll have to think. Scrabble isn't really that exciting to everyone," he said.

"Oh, I don't know. It's exciting the way you tell it," Mom said. Such a typical Mom response.

"And don't forget *funny*," I smiled, as I took another mouthful of Coney. If we were talking about me representing my class, and giving the speech in front of the whole school, I'd be too nauseous to have another bite. But this was Lucas. He would be as relaxed in an auditorium as he was around the table.

"And what about your best-worst, Josie?

"I'd say track practice for both."

"Here, have some salad," Mom said, and passed the bowl. I'd stopped trying to tell Mom that "salad" was more than just a bowl of green leaves, so I was surprised when I saw a Caesar salad tonight.

"Wow, you went all out, Mom. Maybe this dinner is the best thing about today," I said, as I hunted around the bottom for some croutons. Mom's Caesar only had two extra ingredients, croutons and cheese, but that was a huge step up from chopped leaves and dressing.

"I'll take that. So, tell me about the practice."

"Oh, it was just hard trying to hit these times exactly. So that was the worst," I said.

"So, what was the best?" Lucas asked.

"I got close to hitting *one* of these times," I said, pointing to my hand. "Oh, and Mr. B. stretching is second best."

"What was your best and worst, Mom?" Lucas asked.

"Well, the worst thing was that I forgot my hat when I did that roof inspection today. I think I burned my nose a little," Mom scrunched her face. "And up until five minutes ago, the best thing was getting the contract for a new building going up, but now ... being complimented about this meal is most *definitely* the best thing." Mom chuckled.

"Are we going to the hospital after dinner?" Lucas asked, and I kicked his foot.

"Hey!" He scowled at me.

"Josie!" Mom said. Then she answered Lucas. "No, honey. Not tonight."

I crunched on a crouton and tried not to look too relieved.

"Aw. I was going to do my speech for Dad," Lucas said, sticking his bottom lip out.

"He's just tired, honey. And he figures you have homework, or other things to do," Mom said. I scraped up the last few bits of salad and finished my water.

"Maybe I can Facetime him after dinner?" Lucas asked.

"I'm sure he'd love that," Mom said.

"Are you done?" I asked Mom, as I stood up with my plate and reached for hers.

"Yes, honey. Thanks."

"Can I be excused?" Lucas asked.

"Did you have any salad?" Mom asked him.

"Yes! You never see me eating green stuff!" Lucas said, as he got up from the table. "But I do!"

"Okay," Mom said, sounding like she didn't believe him, and also a little tired herself.

"He did. I saw," I said from the kitchen. I put plates in the dishwasher, and Lucas set his plate on the counter.

"Hey, don't be afraid of the dishwasher," I said.

"You're right there."

"I'll get out of your way," I said, grabbing my phone.

I went upstairs to change, and lay down on my stomach, my arms hanging off my bed. I took a picture of my hand and texted Dad the word "Impossible." I did another search for Aurora, and was reading about her, when Mom leaned on my door.

"How much homework do you have?"

"I don't really have any," I said. For some reason, Mom took this as an invitation to come right in, and stood there with her hands on her hips.

"How can that be?"

"I just have to read an article and answer a few questions. I finished everything else in class."

"Hmm. Can you put your phone down?"

"Okay. What?" I asked and sat up.

"Maybe you could review notes, or read ahead in something?"

"There's nothing to review, so I don't really see the point."

"The point is to do more than the bare minimum."

"School is almost over, and my grades are fine," I said, getting annoyed.

"Are they as good as they could be, though?" Mom asked, crossed arms challenging me.

"You make me sound useless or something."

"It's just the opposite! You are very bright, and you cannot tell me you're working your hardest, or to your potential," Mom said.

"I am!"

"I disagree. You whip through homework, and then you're on your phone. Look at the effort you put into running."

"Well, yeah ... because I like it."

"I get that. But you can see how, with running, you put in the effort, and it pays off. And I am so proud of you for that ... I'd just like to see you try a little harder at school, give a little extra."

"Fine. So, can I go downstairs now and read that article?" I got up and walked past her. She sighed as she followed me, and I knew she just had to get the last word in.

"I originally came up here to see what homework you had, and to see if you wanted to watch something later," she said, as she followed me down the hall.

"I could do that," I said, heading down the stairs. For once, her last word wasn't so bad.

"Great," she said, coming downstairs after me. "I have a roof design to finish up. Do what you have to do, and maybe go over something else from today?"

"Okay. Could you make popcorn for when we watch our show?"

"Could you do some extra?"

"Yes, I could," I said, as I took the binder out of my knapsack.

"It's a deal. I'll make the popcorn in a little while," Mom said.

"Did you say popcorn?" Lucas asked, swivelling around with a huge smile.

CHAPTER 16

"THIS GIRL"

When I told Mom I had a practice before school, I left out the part that I was doing it on my own. I really didn't want to get into another conversation about where I put my effort. For me, there was no option. I had four days until Citys, and I wanted to try to hit these times. I sent Dad a second text before bed, but his response was pretty short, and really not that helpful. So, with Dad out of coaching mode, I was really on my own, and had to give Ms. Starter's—Aurora's—times another try.

I figured there'd be some sort of practice going on at the high school, but I wasn't expecting a group of chatterbox Moms working out so early on a Friday morning. I put my knapsack on a bench, set my watch, and started an easy jog around the track. I was joined by the bootcamp Moms for one lap: some fast, some shuffling, some just walking and talking. Mom would've fit in with that last group for sure.

Dad would've insisted on at least a ten-minute warm-up run, but after seven minutes, I just wanted to get started. The ladies were back by the bleachers, and I had the track to myself. I took a sip of water and looked at my hand.

$$300 = 63$$
$$800 = 2{:}48$$
$$400 = 1{:}24$$
$$200 = 42$$

I didn't know if the order mattered, but I figured Aurora wrote it that way for a reason. She was an Olympian, after all, and I'd never even made it to City Finals before.

I walked partway around the track, to where I'd started the 300 yesterday. I imagined myself running around the track. This time, I set my watch to 63 seconds, knowing that I needed to cross the finish line exactly when the alarm went off. Not a second before or after. *I need Dad to help me,* I thought. I still had no clue how to pace myself, and didn't think I could do it without his help. I must've looked strange standing there, staring into space, and it was embarrassment that finally got my butt in gear.

I crouched down, put my finger on my watch, tapped the timer, and ran. I started counting the seconds to myself, but it was too confusing, so I stopped after ten seconds, and just charged. I turned off the timer as I crossed the finish. I went too fast this time. *How the heck do I get this right?* I walked back to where I'd started, caught my breath, took a one-minute rest, and tried again. And again. I was all over the place. Too fast, too slow. I was not getting it. I pulled my shirt up to wipe the sweat from my forehead, noticing the ladies stretching on their mats. *Would anyone mind if I curled up into a ball?*

I went to get water and check texts. Still nothing from Dad. *He must be really tired,* I thought. Or maybe forgot to charge his phone. I texted him, saying I was at the track again. Then I put my bottle down and headed to the start line and. I decided to skip the 800-metre and do the 400-metre. So much for sticking to Aurora's order.

I tried to remember things Dad and I would do when he helped me practice. We did some interval training a few times, top speed sprinting, mixed with light jogging in between. He'd say things like:

"Breathe!"

"Arms!"

"You're wobbling like a bobblehead!" That always made me laugh. He told me what I needed to hear and, even when he teased me, it was always followed by a hug or a kiss on my head. Sometimes he'd hold my face, look me dead in the eye, and say things. But what was it he said? I needed to hear those words, but I couldn't pull them out. I pleaded with my memory. Why couldn't I remember? Maybe when Lucas was talking about Gigi, this was what he meant about remembering. I told him it didn't matter if he forgot things, but it did.

I remembered one important thing, and that was how I wasn't giving up. Dad always told me to finish what I started. I set my watch timer to 1:24. The 400m was the dreaded sprint to some, but it was my comfort zone. I'd gotten close to 1:24 yesterday. I took a minute break, squeezing my waist as I bent over to breathe. I ran it a few more times, until my legs felt like noodles. What training did Prosciutto girl do to be so strong? Was today's workout going to help me at all? Aurora said it would be frustrating, but she didn't tell me I'd be so beat. I really wanted to bail, and thought about what Aurora would do. *She kept running after she fell and wrecked her knee—*

what do you think she'd do?! I knew caving in to a little exhaustion wasn't the Aurora way.

I got another drink and ran the 200-metre, again and again. I didn't ever match the times on my hand, but I came close. After a short cool down, some high school kids arrived, and I went to get my stuff and check my phone. Nothing, so I texted him, "Just finished. Not bad."

I walked across the field to school, snacking on a chewy granola, passing kids and people going to work. I thought it was a pretty good morning, and gave myself a gold star for trying. I'd talk to Dad about it later. I wanted him at the meet, but I really wanted him to get out of the hospital to help me practice this weekend. What I really *needed,* though, was to get to school and change, because I felt pretty gross. I suddenly clawed at my knapsack in a panic. I shifted notebooks and crumpled papers, and there it was: my Old Spice Wolfthorn deodorant. *Phew!!*

CHAPTER 17

"*GUIDING LIGHT*"

After school, Mom drove me to the hospital, before bringing Lucas to Mo's Monkey Obstacle. I was excited to tell Dad about my morning practice. He'd texted me during the day that "it can only get better." *Maybe he actually will get out over the weekend and can come to the track,* I thought.

When Mom pulled in front of the hospital, Lucas slapped the back of my seat.

"Josie, remember, I haven't told Dad about my speech yet."

"I think I got it the first 10 times, Lucas."

"You exaggerate."

"At least I don't repeat myself." I laughed as I got out of the car.

"Tell Daddy we'll pop by after Mo's, and see you at home," Mom said through the window. "And there are leftovers in the fridge."

"Got it!" I half-waved with my back to the car, and walked into the hospital.

As I walked down the hall, I heard an awful howling. It took a minute to realize it was coming from Dad's room. I froze. *What the heck is going on in there? Are they doing tests?* No way did I want to see what the nurse or doctor were doing to him. The sound went from human to hyena and, as I took a step closer to the door, he shouted, "Stop!" So I did. A second later, he burst out laughing.

"And then you puked in your cap!" Okay. He was *not* talking to a nurse or doctor, but who? I figured he was on the phone, but I wanted to know what was going on. So I lingered. Call it nosey.

"Oh, yeah! Sneaking out to the pool ... no sleep ... smoking, and we still kicked ass!!" Smoking? What? He said smoking! When Dad got cancer the first time, he said he'd never been a smoker. Had he lied?? A nurse came around the corner, so I pretended I was texting.

Had she ever heard Dad like this before?

"Oh, you know ... I'll be fine. Been down this road once already ..." Dad said. He had calmed down, so I couldn't hear as well as when he was going ballistic. I got closer to the door, and I heard phrases like "resistant to treatment" and "concerned but hopeful." Mom and Dad talked vaguely about tests, so I was hoping for more details, but I was getting more uncomfortable as more people walked by. I headed into Dad's room, acting as cool as possible, which, of course, meant looking at my phone.

"And here she is now," Dad said, wiping his eyes. He waved me over and tapped his cheek. I gave him a quick peck as he took my hand.

"Almost fourteen. Oh, *just* like me! Hah! No, no ... she's definitely her own person." Dad laughed and stuck his "one minute" finger in the air. I sat down and noticed a few more cards on the side table. St. Peregrine wasn't anywhere to be seen.

"I'd love that. Love you, too. Keep the faith. *Ciao*." Dad tapped his phone.

"You used to smoke?" I blurted out. So much for acting cool.

"What else did you hear, hey?" Dad laughed.

"Avoiding the question, *hey*?" I replied.

"I tried it a few times, but I wouldn't say I smoked."

"So, trying doesn't count as smoking?" I asked. Dad smiled and leaned back.

"Obviously, it *is* smoking, but I wasn't a smoker. Not like some of my old roommates. It's like someone who's gone running a handful of times, probably doesn't call themself a runner." Dad raised his eyebrows and smiled. He had me there.

"Still ... you kind of left that out. Do the doctors know?"

"Yes, honey ... but that really didn't change anything." Dad pulled his covers higher as he shifted in the bed.

"So, what else did you hear?" he asked.

"Not much," I giggled. "I thought you were being tortured, or they were doing tests, and I was not about to come in!"

"Ah, it was just some good old reminiscing." Dad smiled and shook his head. He looked up to the ceiling and bit his lip. "We had so much fun. Now we live all over the place, but I can't tell you how fortunate I feel to have such great friends. I'm so grateful," Dad said. His eyes looked glassy again.

"I get it," I said, though I wasn't sure I did.

"Yeah, like you and Bird and Sofia. You've been friends for so long, and you'll have a lot more adventures together. You're just getting started," he chuckled.

"Uh-huh," I said, thinking of what we would be doing at the fair tomorrow night. I wasn't sure where this conversation was going. I wanted to hear about the puking-in-the-hat thing, and I had questions about what I'd heard him say about treatments, and getting out of the hospital. And, of course, I wanted to talk about my practice. Dad pressed on the tape of his IV and looked up at the hanging bag. The veins in his hand looked like they were pushing up on his skin.

"Does that thing hurt?"

"No, I'm used to it." He smiled like it wasn't a big deal.

"Do you think you'll get out soon?" I asked.

"Oh ... I don't know yet, sweets. They did say something about me going home for a little while, and coming back in for tests. I think they just want to keep an eye on me and try some things out."

"Oh. Well, because I did those drills again ..."

"Yeah, your text sounded like it was better?"

"Kind of."

"You'll get it, eventually, sweetheart."

"I just … I still need your help." I circled the numbers with my finger. I had written over them earlier, and the ink was fresh and dark.

"… I wish I could," he said. "Just keep at it; you'll get there."

"But I'm talking about now. It's Friday and the race is Tuesday! I only have three more days to train." *Alone*, I thought. I could feel tears welling up. I pressed on my thumbnail to stop myself.

"Listen, I'm hoping to be at the race. Okay? Come here." He shifted his legs over and patted the bed. I sat next to him, and he hugged me with his non-IV arm.

"Give it another try over the weekend. It might be better, but it's okay if it's not. It is not easy, sweetheart."

"Okay. Probably in the morning; I'm going to the Bird's tomorrow afternoon, for a sleepover."

"Oh, that's great," Dad smiled.

"Should be fun," I said.

"I have to lie back," he said, and settled down against the pillow. I stood up to give him room, but he still had my hand. He squeezed it and let out a sigh.

"I was reading about Aurora Osborne. I knew about her injury, of course, but she's done some really interesting things in her life. A lot of work with kids," Dad said.

"That's cool."

"Sure is. My girl ... coached by an Olympian. Doesn't get cooler than that." He closed his eyes and, a few minutes later, he was asleep.

CHAPTER 18

"I RAN"

Rain, already, I thought, looking at the grey Saturday morning sky. Rain wasn't going to ruin my run, but it would ruin my night at the fair. Dad and I ran plenty of times in the rain. His theory was, if I could train in crappy weather, I'd have no problem racing in it. We used to jog along the ravine trails that cut through the city, and get home soaked, with mud splattered up the backs of our legs. Dad would say we got *Jackson Pollock-ed,* after the abstract artist.

I planned on running to the track at the high school as a long warmup, and I'd brought my metro card to come home. It was only two stops, but if I got soaked and tired, I wanted an easy out. Standing on the front porch, I chewed my last bite of bagel with peanut butter, and checked my playlist. I clicked on "Back Down," put my phone and card in a Ziploc, and was off.

I looked for Gigi when I was nearing the corner, but all her windows were closed. The relief Lucas felt, seeing her lean out her window, reminded me how his mind was always ticking, and how I often forgot to think about things. A teacher told Mom once that she could see the curiosity bubbling when he spoke. All that Wikipedia reading, I guessed.

The Arkells' "11:11" played as I jogged past apartment buildings, Linda's Nails, Chacho's Restaurant, and wove around people walking their dogs, their kids, themselves. I began to doubt if doing the drills again would help much, especially on my own, but I'd told Dad I would do it. *I'll get it eventually.* I crossed the street and wished Dad would be at the track to help. He was tired and having tests, but I still wanted him with me. It was totally selfish.

I slowed down as the sidewalk got more crowded, and passed by a mix of cafés, restaurants, and stores. I thought back to Dad talking to his friend on the phone.

He was so outrageous, the way he was talking, and not just the smoking bombshell. It was the way he sounded. Loose and—honest. That was it. He seemed so honest, talking to his friend. Even when I couldn't hear him all that clearly, his tone was sincere. And what he said about smoking wasn't anything new to his friend, just to me. It just kind of threw me. Plus, I didn't know what some of the things meant. And when he got quieter ... is that why I felt something was missing?

I rounded the corner by the station when thunder boomed. Rain wasn't the problem, but lightning brought it to a different level. I ran into the station to try to decide what to do: track or home, track or home? I didn't want to get all the way to the high school and get caught in a thunderstorm. I checked the weather on my phone, and sure enough, there was a little cloud with a lightning bolt, and 100% underneath it. Doofus. Why hadn't I checked this before? I bagged the practice, bagged my phone and earbuds in the Ziploc, and made a run for it back home.

The rain drizzled as I cut down a tree-lined side street, past houses, able to run faster with less people around. A flash of lightning, and then thunder about ten seconds later. I clutched my phone in the Ziploc, hoping it was safe. I was a few blocks from home, strands of hair sticking to my face, when I heard the familiar shouting. I bolted for the corner, coming alongside Gigi's building, and when I looked up, there she was, arguing with the thunderstorm. *I so wish I understood you,* I thought.

While I waited for the light to turn, Gigi continued to curse the clouds. Or that's what I suspected she was doing. I wondered what made her like this. All the shouting. What was so important that she had to blast it from her window? I was getting wetter and wetter but I knew I couldn't do anything about the rain, except run home, when the light turned green. Maybe Gigi knew that she had no control over the rain, either, but she could yell at it all she wanted. *I wish I could shout with you.*

I practically knocked the door down when I got home.

"Lucas! I saw Gigi!" I called out. My running shoes squished as I shifted to take them off.

"You did?" he asked, like he was half-happy, and half-sad he missed her.

"She sounded really pissed at the storm," I laughed.

"Aw, you're lucky," he said as I went upstairs to change.

When I came back down, I'd just gotten comfy on the couch, when Lucas wedged himself next to me.

"I'm glad you're home. Can you help me with an assignment?" he asked.

"Ask Mom."

"She's at work."

"She's in her room," I said.

"Yeah, *working!* When she's at her desk, she's at work, and we can't disturb her. Plus, I need you."

"Ugh, I need to relax!"

"You're on your phone," he said, leaning in, a chunk of hair falling in front of his face.

"Yeah, *relaxing!*" I said, moving the pillow behind me.

"Please, Josie! I have to describe how to do one of my favourite things."

"Like annoying me?"

"Not funny."

"So, what then? Parkour ... or reading?"

"You can't describe reading. That's dumb. I'm doing it on camping. Well, putting up a tent, actually. But I need to practise doing it, so I can write about it clearly."

I dropped my phone on my lap and pointed outside. "Uuuh ... it's raining."

"Uuuh," he said, imitating me, "I already thought of that. We can do it in the garage."

"I'm so comfortable, though," I whined.

"Please? I'm supposed to do something that has special meaning to me." He sprang to the floor and leaned on my knees. His blue eyes scored a direct hit. I sat up with an exaggerated sigh, and went to slip on my Birks.

"Okay, okay ... let's make it snappy," I said.

CHAPTER 19

"LITTLE GIANT"

"I'm getting wet again for you. You owe me," I said, as we ran out to the side door of the garage. Lucas peeled a strip of grey paint, while I rammed my shoulder against the door to open it. It smelled like warm dirt inside. I flicked on the light, and it seemed I was looking at everything through a hazy filter of dust. Lucas closed the door and took my arm, while I peered at things that hadn't been touched in years: the leaf blower, weed whacker, saw, orange extension cord. And the power washer. Dad blasted everything with that thing when he first bought it.

"Yeesh. Where's the tent?" Lucas asked.

"Probably in here," I said, opening the cupboard door

where the dusty blue and grey bag lived. I dragged it out and Lucas grabbed a handle.

"Come on. Let's move this stuff to make room, but away from the mouse-poo corner," I said.

"It was a rat. And remember the dead chipmunk?" Lucas asked.

"Mom freaked," I laughed, thinking I might still have the video of her cleaning it up.

We moved bikes and tubs out of the way, and Lucas slid the bag to the cleared area. I took out a camping chair and sat down, while he laid out poles and pegs, and unrolled the light blue fabric. Lucas squeezed in next to me, and listed all the parts in his notebook. I checked the weather on my phone, and saw that the rain was supposed to stop by the afternoon. *No rain at the fair. Phew.*

■

Thunder cracked.

"Yikes!" Lucas said with a quiver in his voice. "Okay. Can you pull this corner over there?" he asked, walking backwards with one side of the tent. He flattened it all out and wrote in his notebook. I held the centre up, while he slid a pole through the slots and into the grommets at both ends, repeating the action with the second pole, and forming a perfect dome. The rain sped sideways past the windows, as we pulled the corners out a little further. I got one of the rolled-up sleeping mats out of the cupboard, and threw it inside the tent.

"You're going in?" Lucas asked, as lightning flashed through the garage-door windows.

"Well, I'm not going out in *that,*" I said, pointing to the rain as I crawled inside.

"Awesome!" Lucas cheered as he followed me.

"Hey! There are still some pine needles in here," he chuckled. "Isn't this so great?"

"Yeah. Even smells a little woodsy," I smiled.

"Dad was happiest when we went camping," Lucas said.

"He sure did love it," I said, thinking about our camping trips. We hiked and swam and ate around a fire. Dad would barbeque hot dogs, but Mom would bring quinoa salads and shrimp cocktail from a frozen ring. Shrimp and quinoa in the woods was beyond wrong.

"Yeah, but he *actually told* me, they were the best times of his life."

"He did? But we only went twice. And Mom hated it."

"I know, but he still loved it ... so I love it," Lucas said, in a way that meant no one was ever going to change his mind.

"Well, me, too! Hey, we need music," I said, pulling my phone from the back pocket of my shorts. Lucas bounced up to his knees, and rested his arm on my shoulder.

"How many playlists do you have?"

"Just a few."

"Can I see?" I tilted my phone in his direction. "No country ... and no singing!" he said, like he was disgusted.

"Hey!" I pushed him on his butt. He got back up and looped his arm through mine. "Do that again and I'll take you with me!" Lucas leaned in again and watched as I scrolled.

"Oh, 'Hey Joe' is a good one," I said.

"The band is called Caamp? Yeah, play it!!" Lucas said. The song had barely started when Lucas's eyes widened.

"Maybe Dad can take us camping this summer?"

"Maybe," I said, my mind on Dad, and wondering what tests he might have to do. I wasn't sure what that meant for planning trips, or even if he'd be at my race.

"We could be real hardcore, without Mom. Even do a canoe trip!"

"I don't know about that." I brushed some of the pine needles into a little pile by the edge of the tent.

"But that would be so fun!" Lucas said.

"Yeah, but ... we have to see how Dad feels." I really didn't know what I was trying to say.

"He'll want to go!"

"He will, but we don't know if he'll be well enough." The phrase "resistant to treatment" flashed in my mind. What exactly did that mean? What treatment? I shifted on the mat and picked up some pine needles, breaking them in half.

"Well, then, if we can't go this summer, then next summer."

"Maybe."

"Do you think he's going to need an operation again?"

"I don't know, Lucas." I sat on my knees, trying to get comfortable.

"When my friend's grandma had lung cancer, she had just one lung. And then she moved really slowly. She was already too old to run, though. And then she died."

"Come on, let's take this down," I said, turning off my phone and crawling out of the tent. The idea of Dad with one lung, or worse—the doctors not being able to do anything for him—made me want out of the garage, out of the conversation.

"Wait. Are you mad at me?" Lucas asked, peeking out of the tent.

"No, I'm just hungry," I lied. Lucas crawled out of the tent.

"But you look mad. Dad could still run with one lung you know. If that's it."

"It's not. I'm fine," I said, sliding one of the poles out of the tent.

"I know my questions annoy you, sometimes." Lucas pulled on the other pole and folded it up in the bag.

"I'm used to it," I said, forcing a smile.

"I just wonder about stuff, like, what's going to happen."

"Well, maybe you don't have to wonder so much. They'll tell us," I said. Lucas picked up the unused pegs and put them in the bag, while I bent down to fold the tent. There was so much of Dad's conversation I didn't get.

"But what if they haven't told us everything?" Lucas asked. And there it was. Lucas got it exactly. That was the niggling question I had floating around my head. *What aren't they telling me?* I stood, holding the tent, and turned to put it in the bag. A tear dripped onto Lucas's T-shirt, and he hung his head. I dropped the tent and hugged him, his body shaking.

"What if Dad ...?" he sobbed. "What if he can't go camping, ever?"

"I don't know. I ..." I felt the sting of tears, but if I cried, Lucas would be more worried. I had to say something to get him, to get us, back to how we'd felt inside the tent.

"Daddy's strong," I said as I kissed his head.

"I know," Lucas murmured.

"And you're strong," I said, giving him a squeeze. Lucas sniffed and started nodding.

"It'll be okay," I said, trying to comfort him and convince myself. "I hope there's no boogers on me," I said.

"There's snot," he said, and started to laugh.

CHAPTER 20

"*I GOTTA FEELING*"

The June Fair was a major event in our part of the city—a celebration of good weather and the school year ending, with all the junk food imaginable. Or, at least, that's what it was to us. We went every year, spending the day on rides, playing games, eating cotton candy and snow cones, and crashing by late afternoon. The past few years, I was allowed to go with friends, but Mom would always be there with Lucas, so it wasn't total freedom. And I was *never* allowed to go at night. Mom thought it was too dangerous. She actually used words like "hooligans and hoodlums" or "shenanigans and tomfoolery." So, knowing Mom would never let me, I did the only thing

I could do—I asked to sleep at Bird's, and said nothing about the fair.

"I can't believe you kiss your parents with that lying mouth of yours!" Bird said when I got to her house.

"I did *not* lie," I said, trying to act offended.

"Avoided the truth, then."

"Yerp!!" I laughed, and then caught a whiff. "Oh my God, your mother's chicken smells so good!"

"Come upstairs first, then we'll eat. Sofia has major plans for you," Bird said. I groaned, and tried to whack her as we went upstairs, but just caught her on the calf.

"Yay!! You're here!" Sofia put down the eyeliner and hopped up to grab me.

"Okay, relax."

"I can't! Time for some mascara on those gorgeous lashes!" Sofia said, clapping her hands.

"Not too much," I insisted, as I hugged a post of Bird's bed.

"Makeover for messing up the experiment. That was the deal," Bird said, like she was some mob boss.

"Hardly a real makeover, just a tiny bit of mascara. You're already pretty," Sofia said.

"You are one soft Danish pastry, Sofia!" Bird said.

"She's just sweet. Thanks, Sofe. I am in your hands!" I said, pushing my flyaway hair back, as I sat on Bird's flowery bedspread. Sofia bent down and got to work.

"Yeah, I know. Since kindergarten. Sofia's the sweet pastry, I'm the chorizo, and you're the string bean!" Bird said, in a variety of accents.

"Bird! Stop making us laugh. I don't want to poke Josie in the eye."

"I know mascara is *muy importante,* but try to make it quick. My mom left us the chicken in the oven, so we'll eat and go. I have to text my brother when we're on our way," Bird said.

"So, what's he getting us?" I asked.

"Something cheap," Bird said.

Sofia put the mascara away and led me to the mirror.

"See? So feathery! This is going to be such a fun night!" Sofia squeaked. I leaned in to look. Not bad.

"Looks great. Let's eat, and then get out of here!" Bird said.

■

The fair was packed. It was starting to get dark and the lights from the rides and carnival games flashed colours all around. I smelled popcorn and cotton candy, and a hint of grease. There were a ton of high school kids. I saw a girl that reminded me of the Whippet, which reminded me of Prosciutto girl, but I pushed away the idea of the meet. The fair was all about fun, not getting nervous about City Finals.

Bird's brother wasn't answering her texts, so we went on a few rides. Just as we came off the spinning swing ride, I froze, and yanked on Bird and Sofia's arms.

"Look! It's Mr. B. and his girlfriend!" I said, pointing toward the duck-shooting game. Mr. B. was holding a huge stuffed dog, standing behind his girlfriend, who was aiming at innocent fake duckies.

"*What* ... is ... he ... wearing?" Sofia asked.

"I'd say a white T-shirt and jeans," Bird said.

"But, why?" Sofia looked like she was about to cry. "He looks so boring. Like anyone else. No colour, no individuality, no ... *flare!*"

"Let's go say hi," I said.

"I don't think I can," Sofia said.

"And, wait! My brother just texted. He wants us to go to the dunk tank. We can go that way," Bird pointed.

We started to speed walk toward Mr. B. on our way to the dunk tank.

"Hi, Mr. B.!" Bird and I said. Sofia just waved.

"Hello, ladies! Having a good time?"

"We are. Nice dog," I said, slowing down.

"Just heading to the dunk tank," Bird said and took my hand.

"Okay! Have fun!" Mr. B. waved. His girlfriend never took her eye off the duck target.

We got to the dunk tank just before Bird's brother did. He teased us and passed a plastic bag to Bird, who stuck it in her drawstring bag. We gave him money and giggled through our goodbyes, then walked past the game stalls to the trees near the outer edge of the park. We kept looking over our shoulders, even though it was pretty dark where we were.

"We've got to be fast," Sofia said, as Bird cracked the bottle open. Keeping the bottle in the bag, Bird took a silent sip, scrunching up her nose. She passed the bottle to me, and around it went.

"Aaack! It burns my throat!"

"I don't have the lady balls for this!"

"I bet our experiment water would've tasted better!" I laughed as I passed the bottle.

"I don't feel anything, do you guys feel anything?" I asked.

"Maybe a little." Bird let out a snort and we all laughed. I wasn't sure what the stuff was supposed to do, but I really didn't feel any different, so I swigged some more. The taste was pure chemical. My tongue wanted to retreat, but I gulped down another swallow. This was not like the tiny sips we took from Bird's parents' booze cabinet. The bottle went around again.

"Bird, Bird, Bird ..." Sofia's finger pecked at Bird's arm. "Does your brother have a girlfriend?"

"Whaaaaat?" Bird screeched.

"He's just sooo ..." Sofia started.

"Don't even!" Bird's hand flew up, and that did it. I roared with laughter, and the giggles just grew from there.

"I thought you were just goofing around when you hid those notes in his room!! He's disgusting! Have you ever watched him eat?" Bird started to make snorting sounds, and we cracked up.

"Guysh-guysh," I said, pawing their arms.

"You're slurring," Bird laughed.

"Mmm not." I looked at my two best friends, and threw my arms around them. "You know what? I love you guys!"

"Aw, love you, too," Bird said.

"Me, too," Sofia said.

"We've been friends for how many years?" I asked.

"Please do *not* make me do math right now," Sofia begged.

"Eight years, nine months, and seven days," Bird said.

"Are you kidding me?" Sofia asked, with a look of disbelief on her face.

"Yes, I'm kidding! I mean, I know it's eight years, I just guesstimated the rest!" Bird laughed.

"That's what I mean. We've been best friends for sooo long," I said, thinking about all I'd been through with them. We liked different things, but we loved each other for those differences.

"And you guys are always helping me," Sofia added.

"Oh my God, Sofe, you help me, too. I'm sorry I messed up the filter!" I put my forehead to hers.

"It's okay! I'll still do better than I normally would," Sofia said.

"You worked just as hard as us, maybe more," Bird said. We hugged and laughed, and petted each other's hair. Their faces reflected the coloured lights from the rides. We complimented each other, until it got gross and goofy.

"I love you guys sooo much. You are the best friends on the planet. And you know what? We'll be friends forever." I pulled them in closer.

"So deep, and so true!" Bird teased.

"Hey, I can see the hospital from here," Sofia said.

"Barely," Bird said.

"Does your dad have a view? Maybe he can see the pretty lights of the fair," Sofia said.

"He doesn't," I said, feeling my stomach tighten.

"Drop it," Bird said to Sofia, and I turned to walk toward the trees.

"What did I say?" I heard Sofia ask, and then Bird whispered something as they caught up to me.

"It's fine, guys," I said, and wished it felt true.

"I didn't mean to upset you, Jose. I'm sure he'll be okay ..." Sofia said.

"Of course, he will!" Bird said, like it was obvious, but I wasn't so sure how obvious it was.

The question Lucas asked in the garage had scared me, because I really had no answers. What weren't they telling me? Dad said things to his friend on the phone, but not to me. Parents want to protect their kids. What was I missing? I closed my eyes to stop the tears, then just sat on the ground, and covered my face. Bird and Sofia plopped right down next to me.

"I'm mmm, sorry," I blubbed. "I don't want to ruin it ... ruin our fun. Sss ... sorry."

"Don't be sorry," Bird said. Each one had an arm around me.

"What is it?" Sofia asked.

"I just wish ... I wish I knew what was happening."

"It must be hard, but they'll figure it out," Sofia said.

"They're doing tests, but nobody really tells me or *explains* anything. So, I'm clueless. Even Lucas is figuring things out ... just today, he told me he's been wondering what's going to happen."

"Maybe there's nothing to tell," Bird said. I shook my head back and forth. I was afraid to say it, but it was right there.

"But there is. I ... oh, I just think ..." I tried.

"What is it?" Sofia asked.

"I think ... he might die this time." I slid my hand under my nose to wipe the snot and tears, and hung my head. Bird and Sofia got closer. Quiet. What could they say? I wasn't sure how long we stayed in the huddle. I had stopped crying, but my head throbbed.

"Umm, Josie. I can't even imagine how bad this is for you. And I'm sorry I started this, but ... umm ... and I don't mean to sound insensitive again, but my butt is kind of damp. Can we stand up?" I looked at Sofia's sweet face, looking so sad.

"Mine, too," I laughed. "I'm actually soaked!" Then they all laughed with me.

Standing was harder than I thought. Everything spun. Bird and Sofia took me by each arm.

"Wait a minute," Sofia said. "I've got to clean your eyes. You look like a baby panda." She pulled the sleeve of her hoodie, licked it, and reached toward my face.

"Eew, no! You're like my Mom!" I said.

"Hold still," she said, as she wiped under my eyes. "Better."

We held hands, and weaved in and out of the crowd. The noise, motions, and colours seemed bigger, wilder. I felt like I was wearing a hat that was too big, that made my head flop around. I couldn't handle the wavering feeling.

"Keep me away from the yellow duckies," I said.

"What?" Bird and Sofia asked.

"I don't want to see Mr. B. like this."

"Don't worry, we'll stay clear," Sofia said.

"Bird? Sofe? I don't feel so good."

"Whoa! Okay. Hang on," Bird said.

The ground tilted and I swayed. Or maybe it was the other way around. "I think I'm going to be sick."

"Quick, Sofe, over here!" Bird said, as they pulled me away from the crowd. I tripped on some wires as we went behind a game booth. My body cranked forward and I puked. They both held me. One of them pulled my hair back. I bent over further and hurled again.

"We've got you," Bird said, as I felt two hands on my back, my friends practically holding me up. I puked again and again, until it was finally over.

"Okay. I think I'm done. Yup, I'm done," I said, wiping my mouth. "I think I need some water."

"We'll get you some," Sofia said, and we started to walk back through the games, toward the food stands. I clung to their arms, walking with my head down. Bird and Sofia were talking, but I couldn't really register much more than the sounds of the rides and screams.

"Uh-oh," Bird said as we stopped.

"Wow. Shiny shoes!" I said, still staring at the ground. "Bird, Sofe! What kind of bonehead wears shiny shoes to a fair?" I asked.

"The police kind," Bird said. "Now shut up."

CHAPTER 21

"GIMME SYMPATHY"

Would death have a feeling? I guessed it would feel like a helmet riveted to your skull, while your eyes burned from the inside, and your lips were super-glued shut. That was pretty much how I felt when I woke up. I groaned, but the vibration hurt my brain.

"Hey, there," Mom said, as her cold hand brushed across my cheek. Muffled voices and sounds. The pillow crackled, as I turned toward her and tried to open my eyes.

"Oooh. My head," I squeaked. I reached for Mom's ice-pack fingers and pressed them to my head. Then I opened my eyes. If I wasn't dead, I was about to be, but I really couldn't think past the throbbing.

"Why am I in the hospital?" I moaned. The last time I was here, besides visiting Dad, was for stitches in my finger. I was about eight, and I learned the hard way that even the biggest knife cannot slice a frozen bagel.

"You're okay. What you feel is a hangover. We'll talk it over at home." I looked at her, not knowing what to expect, but seeing an expression I hadn't expected. And she sounded sympathetic. This hangover thing was confusing.

"I gotta pee."

"Okay, hang on, this is coming with you." Mom held my arm with the IV in it, as I swivelled my legs around to sit up. She swept my hair around to my back. I pulled the hospital gown over my thighs, and Mom put my Birks on the floor in front of me. Then she held me, as I slid into my shoes and stood up. I felt a slight breeze, and felt the back of the gown gaping open.

"Can you fix this so I'm not flashing?" I hugged my middle with one arm, as she tied the belt. Then she pushed the curtain from around the bed, and pointed to the bathroom.

As I peed, my brain started to function. My memory of the fair was patchy, and I couldn't remember everything that had happened. Drinking. Laughing. Crying. Barfing. Shiny black shoes. Then nothing. Not good. And what was worse, I didn't know what Mom knew. She was being soft and calm, probably because she wasn't going to rip into me at the hospital. But *consequences* were coming, I just knew it. I needed the missing pieces, but I felt too crappy to even ask her for my phone. I figured that would be pushing it, anyway.

I dragged myself back to the bed and got changed, and before long, they released me to go home. It would've been better slipping out in a disguise, but I had to wait for the doctor to tell me, "Don't do that again," while wearing my vomit-scented top. Mom said she'd tried to clean it, but I could tell she hadn't used soap.

When we got home, I rushed to get out of my pukey top and take a shower. I put on comfy shorts and a T-shirt, crawled into bed, and searched for the coolest spot for my feet. I pulled Mr. Puffy to my cheek, and heard the dull pulsing from my neck echo in the pillow. It was a weird sound, but the steadiness of it was soothing, and made me want to sleep.

"Sit up and drink this," Mom said as she came into my room.

"Later," I grumbled.

"Sit up," she said. Sympathy had left the building. She

handed me a glass of water and put two tablets on my nightstand.

"You can take those around noon if you need. I've got to go pick up Lucas, but before I go, can you please tell me what you were thinking last night?" I set the glass down, and twirled the plastic hospital bracelet around my wrist.

"I don't know. We just wanted to have some fun."

"Fun. Uh-huh. I know we've talked to you about drinking ... and you've rolled your eyes at me when I've said it can be dangerous." Mom dropped her head and shook it. "I don't need to list all the things that could've happened, but believe me, I went through them all. I even wondered if this is how you want to make yourself feel before your race? Anyway, what happened last night is exactly why I harp on things."

"I know."

"And the fact that you didn't ask permission about going to the fair. That's just deceitful." The H between her eyebrows meant she was pissed. The boom of punishment was ready to fall. I looked down, as I pulled the covers to my stomach.

"Do you remember what happened?" she asked.

I told Mom the snippets of what I remembered, then

she piped in. Her voice was monotone, but soft, and luckily, she didn't linger on the major humiliations: the policeman (shiny shoes!), vomiting (how many times?), passing out (like, on the ground?), the crowd (OK, we have to move), the ambulance (now I need to change my name).

"This was so frightening for me. To get that call. To see you in the hospital." Mom's voice was shaky, and I still couldn't look at her. I bit my bottom lip. Drunk and deceitful was probably punishment level 6; terrifying Mom took it to a 9. If she told Dad, it would be off the chart. I braced for a punishment that would last through the rest of my teen years.

"Did you tell Dad?"

"Oh my God, no!" I looked at her, and realized she looked more sad than mad.

"I don't want to see him today," I said.

"Okay. I think you should rest, anyway. I'll text him later."

"Thanks, Mom. Can I ask you something?"

"Sure."

"How long does a hangover last? I mean, will I be okay by Tuesday?"

"Yes, honey. It usually just lasts a day."

"Oh, good. I could never run with this headache." I sighed and put Mr. Puffy in my lap. "I ... I am really sorry, Mom," I said. She took my hand and kissed it.

"Do you remember being upset?" she asked.

"A little." *What does she know?* I thought. I really didn't want to talk about my tear fest, or what I could or couldn't remember.

"You were upset about Daddy," she said. I didn't remember everything, but I remembered the feeling of that truth running into me. I saw the tears in Mom's eyes and, all of a sudden, let mine go. She held my head into her shoulder.

"I know it's scary, honey. And that's because it's not as clear cut as it was before. But you know Daddy ... he is so positive and hopeful," Mom said as she stroked my hair.

"So, what does that mean?"

"It means we stay hopeful, too. It means Daddy is fighting it."

"But how?"

"How? Well, it's hard. Some of it's just fighting his own thoughts and doubts. Being scared makes everything harder. But your dad will do anything he can, because of you and Lucas. He has to be hopeful the doctors will find a way. He has to be positive. And he will not give up."

"Lucas is scared," I said.

"I know. This ..."

"Sucks," I said before she could finish.

"It's the worst. Everything pales in comparison."

I felt the sting rise in my eyes, and my head felt like it was going to explode.

"I'm scared, too, Mom."

"I know, baby," she said and held me tighter. I didn't want to know this truth. It was out of its hiding place now, and I didn't know what to do with it.

CHAPTER 22

"IT'S ALRIGHT, IT'S OK"

I was pretty foggy when I woke up, but as soon as reality clicked, I flung myself out of bed. I needed my phone. I needed to talk to Bird and Sofia. What if there were pictures, or worse—videos? The phone wasn't on my dresser. I figured Mom had it, so I went down to look for her bag by the front door. It wasn't there.

Lucas was sitting right in front of the TV, practically face-to-face with Sponge Bob.

"Have you seen my phone?" I asked. I knelt in between him and his cartoon friends and asked again.

"No! Move! Your breath smells!"

"Uck," I groaned. I headed into the kitchen.

"Hi. How do you feel? You had a good long sleep," Mom said, wiping her hands on a towel. I spotted Mom's bag and sat down beside it.

"Still have a little headache." I tried to sound soft and un-panicky.

"You probably need to eat. I made you chicken soup with pastina. It should tide you over till dinner." She pushed my hair aside and kissed my forehead. Mom knew my favourite comfort food, I had to give her that.

"Um ... Have you seen my phone?"

"I have." Mom put some soup in a bowl and set it in front of me.

"Can I have it?"

"Soon. I have to say, you do get a lot of texts."

"You read them?"

"Well, they kind of filled the screen."

"But they're to me, not you!"

"Hey, I pay. I get to audit."

"Yeah, but you can't just do it without asking me!!"

"Well, I can ..." she said, turning off the stove.

"Mom!"

"Eat that first. And no need to be all snotty with me after last night."

"I really need to talk to Bird." I didn't know if it was the desperation in my voice or what, but she went to her bag and put my phone next to me.

"I did not read your texts, by the way."

"Thank you," I mumbled and took a spoonful of pastina. The good thing about pastina was, you barely had to chew. I texted Bird and Sofia as I inhaled the soup. Luckily, I didn't get anything from Dad, and it was probably guilt that made me avoid texting him. Most of the texts I got were from Bird and Sofia, but there were a few from classmates, checking to see if I was okay. I didn't even remember seeing them at the fair.

The pastina made me feel so much better, and after I ate, I went to the couch to see if there was any fallout on social media. Still no replies from Bird or Sofia. I was starting to get a little antsy.

"What were you and Mom talking about?" Lucas asked as he channel-surfed.

"Nothing."

"It didn't sound like nothing."

"You don't need to know everything."

"I was just asking."

"Well, some things are private," I said. I wanted my

barfing in public to be a private thing.

I was still scrolling when Bird called.

"Just a minute," I said to her as I ran upstairs.

"Oh my God, are you okay?" Bird asked.

"Yeah," I said, lying on my bed with Mr. Puffy at my side.

"Did they pump your stomach?"

"No!"

"That's what some drama-mongers are saying."

"Jeez. No! Nothing like that. I just slept with an IV in my arm." I pushed my pillow behind my head. "Bird, have you seen anything bad about ... it?"

"Not at all. I think some people took pictures when the ambulance came, but I haven't seen any posts."

"I'm going to crawl under a rock!" I pulled Mr. Puffy up to my neck. "And Mr. B. didn't see us, did he?"

"Nope."

"Phew."

"What did your mom say?" Bird asked.

"She has been freakishly chill. So calm."

"Really? I'm waiting for my parents to find out. I told my mother you didn't sleep over, because you got food poisoning from a bad burger."

"Seriously?"

"Hopefully, I'm in the clear." Bird laughed.

"I just hope my dad doesn't find out."

"You think your mom will tell him?"

"No."

"Well, then he won't. Don't worry."

"Yeah. It's just being in the same hospital as him. Not like word is going to get up to him, though," I sighed, trying to remember all that happened. All the things I said.

"Jose, I'm sorry. I should've known you were worried."

"It's okay. You couldn't have known. I …" I was having trouble putting it into words. "I wasn't worried, you know? Not when he went back in. But all these different things made me feel like it's worse than anyone was saying," I said. *And then the fear got me,* I thought.

"I don't know what to say," Bird said softly.

"Me, either. I can't give up hope, though."

"No, you can't. I am here for you, even though I'm not super helpful at the moment."

"I know … and thanks for taking care of me."

"Of course, Dahling," Bird said in one of her many accents. "But hey … you only get to puke on me once."

CHAPTER 23

"HICCUP"

I was pretty sure I'd feel back to normal for the meet, but when I went into the bathroom, the mascara shadow under my eyes made me look like I'd run an all-night marathon. Mom's makeup remover was next to the sink, and when I opened her drawer to look for cotton pads, a complete beauty counter was on display: eye shadows, pencils, lipsticks, mascara, eyelash curler, tweezers, nail files, makeup brushes. I looked at the shadow colours and picked up Mom's go-to eye shadow. It was called "Stray Dog." How was that even a colour? And who thought that was a good name for something to put on your eyes? I sighed. Sofia was the queen of colour and would do a way better job.

After I washed my face, I pulled out the magnifying mirror. *Everything was so huge!* I zoomed in on some blackheads on my nostrils. I squeezed a few, but it was too painful. I noticed a lot of tiny hairs on my face. Most were really faint, but the ones between my brows were dark. Those just had to go. I got Mom's tweezers and plucked, but it made me sneeze with almost every hair I yanked. After getting rid of a few stray hairs under my left brow, I pushed the hairs around with my finger to try to cover the tiny scar where no hair grew. I plucked and pushed others down to fill the space. There had to be a better way. I spotted the razor in the cup, and tossed the tweezers back in the drawer.

■

When I went down to the kitchen, Mom was standing at the counter, about to put dressing on the salad.

"Mom?" I felt my nose tingle, but I wasn't going to cry again. I hung my head so she couldn't see. She'd been so cool and calm about last night. Still, I braced myself.

"What's the matter?"

"Umm. Problem over here," I muttered.

"What kind of problem?" she asked.

"Are you still sick?" Lucas asked as he came into the kitchen.

"No. Could you mind your own business?"

I shuffled around the island, staring down at Mom's jeans and fluffy slippers.

"What's the matter?" she asked. Her spoon clinked on the counter. I clenched my eyes shut, lifted my head, and pulled my hair back like curtains. If my eyes were closed, I couldn't see her reaction.

"Oh, Josie," was all she said. I let go of my hair and opened my eyes. She had her hand on her own forehead, by her own whole, intact, unshaven eyebrows.

"It ... it was an accident."

"An accident?"

"Uh-huh." I wished I could sound more convincing.

"Honey, spare me, please. The ends of your eyebrows are missing," Mom said. In a flash, Lucas came around in front of me.

"Let me see!"

"Go away!" I put my arm out and tipped my hair in my face.

"Why can't I see?"

"Lucas, take the salad to the table."

"Is this one of those teen rebellions?"

"GO A-A-AWAY!" I yelled.

"Josie, don't take this out on him. Lucas, just please go sit down. We'll be right there." Mom turned back to me and pushed my hair off my face. "What were you trying to do?"

"I don't know. I tried plucking but did, like, two hairs, and it hurt and made me sneeze, and the razor was there, so I did a little, but then I had to do the other side to make it even," I said, without taking a breath. "And that just made it worse." I hoped my rambling would somehow make what I did seem more accidental. This was the second mess of the weekend where I really needed my mom. I rested my head and hands on the counter.

"Okay. It'll be all right." Mom rubbed my neck. "Take the chicken, sit down, and start eating. I'll be right back."

"Don't. Even!" I said to Lucas, before he could open his mouth. I took a piece of chicken and started to eat.

"I promise I won't say anything, if you let me see."

"Ugh, you never let up, do you? Fine." My fork clanked on the plate, and I pulled my hair back and added, "But not a word." He didn't have to. His mouth dropped open, like he'd just seen an old guy's wrinkly butt.

"All right. Say something!"

"I thought it was going to be worse?"

"Is that a question?"

"No. I thought they were gone, but it's like you just have mini-moustaches above your eyes," he said, pinching his index finger and thumb together.

"Oh, that makes it better!" I moaned.

Mom came back, carrying an eyebrow pencil and a hairbrush. She sat down and pulled her chair toward me.

"Pull your hair back for me. We're going to do a little magic trick here."

I looked at Lucas, who was munching on string beans. As Mom started to draw, I closed my eyes. I felt her make tiny feathery strokes along the edge of my eyebrow. I smelled garlic on her hands.

"Can I see?"

"In a minute." She brushed all my hair forward and said, "There!" with a laugh. And then, with the corner of the brush, she made a part down the middle, smoothing it on either side. The only time I parted my hair in the middle was when Mom did my French braids for races. And when I was five.

"Now you can look."

I dashed to the mirror by the door. It didn't look that bad, and I skipped over to hug her.

"How long will it take for them to grow back?" Lucas asked.

"A few weeks," Mom said as I sat down to eat.

"Weeks?" I whined.

"What did you think?"

"But I can't ..." I said. Shaved eyebrows combined with the fair fiasco ... it was just too much. "Do I have to go to school tomorrow?"

"Hmm, let me think. No, you should stay home," she said.

"Is that sarcasm?" I asked.

"Yes, that was definitely sarcasm."

"Please, Mom, just one day?" I begged.

"Josie, if anyone notices, you just tell them the truth. Make a joke out of it."

"But it isn't a joke! It's social suicide!!"

CHAPTER 24

"US"

Nothing like wasted angst. I dreaded going to school Monday morning, with my butchered brows, but Bird and Sofia didn't even notice them when I arrived. Their focus must've been on being my own personal bodyguards. They walked on either side of me down the hall, which was kind of overkill, since the fallout from the fair was pretty mild. There'd been some exaggerated stories about my stomach being pumped, but most of the messages or posts showed more concern than nastiness.

After two guys passed me in the hall, doing a stagger and hurl routine, I realized that barf jokes were better with a live audience.

"Grow up!" Sofia sneered, as the next crew of drunken mimes crashed into lockers.

"Just ignore them," Bird said as we locked arms.

"I'm fine," I replied, with a new-found gratitude for my protectors.

"Do boys just think everything is a big joke? Arrgh!" Sofia growled, looking over her shoulder.

"Thanks, my little pit bull." I took Sofia's arm, so the three of us were linked all the way to Drama class.

"See you at lunch. And remember your lady balls," Bird said. "Or just hide behind your guard dog."

"We got this," Sofia said, leading me into Drama, something I'd had enough of the past few days.

■

In the class, I got a few sympathetic smiles from some of the girls. We were told to get into our groups, and finish our masks and scripts. Sofia and I went to a corner to work on our script. I took out my notebook and flipped through the pages. When I looked up, Sofia was staring at me through a golden ringlet. *Uh-oh, she's noticed my eyebrow.* I smoothed my hair along my face.

"You sure you're okay? You look ... kind of *not here.*"

"I'm all right. Just thinking about the race tomorrow," I said. It wasn't a total lie, and easier than exposing my eyebrows. Sofia's bottom lip stuck out and she leaned forward.

"You sure that's all? It's just the stuff you were crying about—I'm sorry I brought up the hospital and upset you," she whispered.

I figured Sofia and Bird must've talked about it over the weekend. I talked with Bird, but should've known a few texts with Sofia didn't mean the conversation was covered.

"It's really, really okay," I said.

"You can talk to us about anything."

"I know. I tell you guys everything," I said. *Almost ...*

"Okay. But, well, this is kind of the biggest *everything* for you right now." Sofia said. All I could do was nod and focus on my mask.

The biggest everything. I thought humiliation from the fair, or ruining my eyebrows was the biggest everything. I remembered when the biggest everything used to be a race. Then it was my parents' divorce, and then Dad's cancer. But then he got better. So why hadn't I thought Dad's getting sick again was the biggest everything? Because he'd kicked it before? Because of the race? Then, somehow, City Finals became the biggest everything. I felt a clench in my stomach, pulling my ribs in. *Is what's happening with Dad going to be the biggest everything ever?*

"Jose, you okay?" Sofia asked. "You're looking a little green."

"Uh-huh." I got my water bottle out of my knapsack and had a swig.

"Maybe you should call your mom."

"No!"

"You're not going to yack again, are you?"

"No, no," I laughed.

"Well, tell me if you do. I promise I'll hold your hair back again."

"You're the best, Sofe. I promise to do the same for you one day."

"I won't be drinking that stuff again!" she said, and we laughed.

At lunch, we found Bird and Lucas outside on our bench. Lucas bopped over to me.

"Josie! Josie! My class voted for *my* speech!"

"Hey! Awesome!" I said, holding up my hand with pride.

"Oh, yeah!" He jumped to give a high-five. "Okay, I gotta go! See you later!" he said with a wave.

"Congratulations, Kookie Lukie!" Bird and Sofia said in unison as he ran off.

"He's just the cutest," Sofia said as we sat down on the bench.

"He is. And how are you?" Bird asked while I was opening my lunch bag. I had just caught the way she looked at Sofia, as if she was unsure what to say.

"Can we please just get back to normal?" I sighed. I took my mortadella sandwich out of the container and bit into it.

"Well, you mowing down your mortadella is normal!" Bird laughed.

"Okay. We don't want to upset you, but we don't want you to crack again, either," Sofia said.

"Crack??!" I asked. "I'm not ... Oh my God! How bad was I?" I asked, waiting for one of them to answer, while kids chattered and ran around us.

"Kind of like your Mr. Puffy doll," Bird finally said.

"Floppy. I know that. No, I mean, how much did I ... *crack?*"

"You were just really, really sad, Josie. And we were sad that we couldn't help," Sofia said.

"But you do," I said, meaning it like it was the truest thing I'd ever said.

"And not to sound all therapist-y, because that's Sofia's department, but we want you to talk to us more about stuff," Bird said.

"No hiding stuff," Sofia smiled.

"Okay. You two have always been there for me." I didn't feel sad or scared, all of a sudden, just lucky.

"And you're always there for us," Bird said.

"Not lately," I said, realizing for the first time how wrapped up I was with Dad and my training.

"It's okay. We take it in turns. You help me when I'm down about school stuff," Sofia said, and bit into her sandwich.

"Or I ruin an experiment." I smiled. Sofia was chewing, and just waved it off with her hand, saying something that sounded like, "Fuhgettaboutit."

"And you know I need you to help me get over my stage fright," Bird said.

"I know," I said, thinking what a good dancer Bird was, and how sad it would be if she was too nervous to perform. I understood the whole being nervous thing ... but the fair and my eyebrows had distracted me from the race. The closer it got to race time, the more anxious I would feel. I felt relieved about seeing Dad later. I just had to keep the ends of my eyebrows covered.

"We've always got your back," Bird said, giving me a hug. "And speaking of body parts ... there's one other part that concerns me." I bit my bottom lip. *Oh crap! Eyebrows.*

"How are your legs?"

"My legs?" I asked. I looked down at my legs, and my untied shoelace.

"Yeah, those things you run with? Going to kind of need them for your big race tomorrow," Bird said, and Sofia giggled.

"I wish I could skip school and come," Sofia said.

"Me, too. I should've jumped farther!" Bird laughed. She shook my shoulder. "You're going to *The Show*, Josie!"

"And you're going to kick butt!" Sofia said, sounding all tough.

I needed to haul myself out of this mood from the *Fair and Eyebrow Zone*. I was going to City Finals for the first time, and I wanted to feel the same excitement my friends had for me.

"And, you know what you need to kick butt?" Bird asked.

"Lady balls!" we all said at the same time.

CHAPTER 25

"HUMAN"

Mr. B. called us to the gym for a quick meeting after school. He wore green pants, a blue shirt, and matching blue shoes. He looked like the earth, and probably got the ocean-to-land ratio about right. I agreed with Sofia. I preferred his colourful outfits to the boring jeans and T-shirt.

I dodged the younger kids, and walked over to stand with the twins. We weren't talking for long, when Mr. B. whistled with his fingers.

"All right, gang. The race schedule is being passed around, so make sure you take one. Tomorrow is *The Show*, and I want everyone to have pasta for dinner. Ask Mom or Dad real nice, or make it yourselves. I've emailed your parents, and we've arranged how you're getting to the meet. You must be there, to warm up, an hour and a half before your race time. I don't need to remind you, we are a team; there aren't as many of us, so bring your big loud selves to cheer for each other. Oh, and also, in bed early. Okay, any questions? No? Good. See you tomorrow."

I picked up my knapsack from between my feet, and was saying bye to the twins, when Mr. B. came up to me.

"How are you feeling, kid?"

"Pretty good. I practised those times again."

"Oh, nice. And did you have fun at the fair?" he asked.

"Yeah," I said, adjusting my knapsack on my shoulder. Bird had assured me that Mr. B. hadn't seen me in my drunken stupor, but I couldn't be sure he hadn't heard rumours.

"Great. So, listen, about tomorrow, I don't want you to put too much pressure on yourself, under the circumstances."

"Uh, I'm not," I said.

"What I mean is, you've done great, so just have fun."

"Okay. Um, I've got to go meet my mom. Thanks, Mr. B.," I said.

"Is she coming tomorrow?" he asked.

"I think so." I walked toward the door.

"Awesome! We sure enjoy her cheering," he smiled. Mom cheered for every kid on the team, even if she didn't know them. I was way past being embarrassed, because so many of them said how nice she was. And she was. She'd always been encouraging, but at the same time, her guttural bellow sounded like she was channelling Darth Vader.

I found Lucas in the playground, and we took the bus to meet Mom at the Running Box. He lit up all over again when he told Mom about his speech being chosen, and she used her track-meet voice to express her excitement. She didn't seem to care that we were inside.

When Mom calmed down, she showed me a few pairs of socks she'd been waving around in her hands.

"How about these?" she asked. Mom knew I needed to inspect and feel the fabric, because of her past botched sock purchases. She claimed I was "fussy," but I just didn't like how thick or bunchy the socks were that she usually bought. Or worse, how the toe seam would bother me.

"Maybe." I rubbed them between my fingers, and traced others on the rack. I thought of Dad's lucky socks that he wore for every meet. I had my lucky shorts, so it wasn't that different, except that my shorts were always clean.

"Can I go look at running shoes?" Lucas asked, then

dropped his knapsack and left before Mom answered. I lifted a mini hanger with a pink pair of socks.

"These feel good." I handed them to Mom; she checked the price and grabbed another pair.

"Let's take two. Or do you want another colour?"

"Oh. No, those are good. Shmanks, Mom."

We went to pay, and it dawned on me that when Mr. B. emailed parents, Mom might've written back and told him about the fair.

"Did you email Mr. B.?" I asked, while Mom tapped her credit card on the machine to pay.

"I responded to his email. Why?" She handed me the socks, called Lucas, and we headed out of the store.

"What did you say?" I asked, as we walked along the street to the car.

"Well, when he emailed all the parents about tomorrow, I just wanted him to know you've been under some stress."

"Geez, Mom! Did you tell him about the fair?" I looked around, thinking I was kind of loud.

"Of course not. I didn't give him specifics."

"Why did you have to say anything?" I couldn't believe that she'd even answered him!

"I just thought he'd be sympathetic, if you're feeling too stressed," Mom said.

"Oh my God! Too stressed? Like I wouldn't race?" I asked, clenching the socks in my hand.

"No, of course not," she said, as we all got in the car.

"Can you two stop arguing?" Lucas asked, and silenced the both of us. I was so annoyed with Mom, but I didn't know how to work through it. Feelings from the fair, feelings about the race were all jumbled.

"Mr. B. kind of requested your cheering," I said.

"Oh, great! I'll have to warm up my voice," she said.

"Well, I don't really want you to," I said, waiting for her reaction.

"You don't want me warming up?"

"I don't want you cheering. That deep voice you use is embarrassing."

"I can use my normal voice."

"I think it's good, how loud you can get," Lucas said.

"And I don't want you being so loud."

"All right, honey. I understand." She reached over and took my hand. "I get you're nervous."

"Noooo!" I pulled my hand away. "I just don't want to hear it, and have it distract me and stress me out even more."

"Okay," she said.

I stayed quiet the whole way to the hospital. Mom and Lucas talked about his swimming lesson, and the things he would probably do. I just couldn't wait to see Dad, and get the pep talk I needed more than ever.

I kept thinking about what had even happened at the store. It felt like one minute, I was picking out socks and feeling good, and within a few seconds, I was mad again. It seemed stupid that Mom emailing Mr. B. flicked a switch that made me want to turn Mom off. It was bad enough Dad couldn't come to the race, and then I silenced Mom. Mom and her booming voice that made me know she was there, rooting for me. I had missed them both at the East Division meet, and it was going to be the same thing at City Finals. And it was my own fault.

CHAPTER 26

"RATHER BE"

The afternoon light coming into Dad's room made it seem grey and bright at the same time, like a filter I'd used to make photos look "artsy." Dad was asleep, facing the window, probably sleeping from boredom. Even his breathing sounded bored. I'd never paid attention to the view, and it didn't get any more exciting when I got to the window, just a roof with metal boxes and pipes a few floors below. Probably like the roofs Mom inspected for her engineering work. But on the road, alongside that part of the building, was a parked ambulance, and I could just see the edge of a sign. Emergency Room. I pressed my head to the window. *Jeez! I really was right under him on Saturday night!*

I sat down and glanced at the flashing numbers and lines that blipped on the screens. I saw those boxes and tubes every time I came to visit, but had no clue what they did. They just meant Dad was okay.

I had been on my phone for a bit, when Dad cleared his throat.

"Hi," I said.

"Hello, my sweetheart," he said, sounding groggy.

"How are you?" I got up to give him a kiss. Pieces of my hair fell forward, so I smoothed them back into place, hoping he wouldn't notice my brows.

"Bit tired, but all right. Grab that thing to sit me up, will you?"

"Sure," I said, and pressed the remote to prop him upright.

"Thanks, babe. Where's your mom and Lucas?"

"Swimming, but he's coming here after to see you."

"Oh, great. I missed you this weekend," he said with a smile.

"Yeah, sorry about that," I said, sliding my hands under my legs. I felt bad, but what was I going to say? *"Sorry, got totally smashed at the fair, and couldn't make it up from the ER."* No way.

"Oh, hey, I get it. So, how are you feeling about tomorrow's race?"

"Fine," I said and shrugged my shoulders.

"Okay," he said slowly. "Come on ..." He looked at me like we both knew he'd get it out of me. For him, it was all about the race, but for me, it was the whole mix. It was a jumbled mess, and I wouldn't have even known where to start. The race was my "biggest everything" at the moment, and I figured all the other stuff could wait until after. I probably wouldn't ever tell him about the fair. It'd bring "freak out" to a whole new level.

I sat on the bed, and Dad lifted his arm around me.

"You've got this, sweetheart," he said, jiggling me slightly.

"Ugh," I groaned.

"No 'ugh.'"

"I don't think I can do it."

"Don't give me that! Who has run with you forever?"

"You."

"So, who knows what you're capable of?"

"You. I suppose."

"And I know you'll do great," Dad said, like a true super-fan.

"You have to say that."

"I'm not saying you'll win again, or that you even have to ... but you'll go out there and give it your all." He drew in a breath, but stopped short, like a hiccup.

"You okay?"

"Yes, yes!" He waved me off. "Listen to me, you've trained extra hard this week ... and you did it all on your own."

"Well, I did have my new drills," I said, smiling.

"Oh sure ... keep reminding me about your new Olympian coach!" Dad teased.

"I don't really think the drills did much."

"Doesn't matter. You tried it. And now, you go do what you do. All your pre-race stuff: have a good breakfast, warm up to your playlist ..."

"... wear my lucky shorts, Mom will do my fast hair ..."

"Exactly."

"Nothing disgusting like you and your lucky socks," I joked.

"Hey, they helped me run fast." He let out a short laugh.

"I know, I know. You had to hide them from Nonna. You've told me that a million times."

"Oh, sorry if I'm repeating myself!" he said, just as the nurse came in.

"Sounds like fun in here, Mr. Tomaselli," she said.

"Always, with my girl," Dad responded. I usually wanted to hide when he said those kinds of things, but I smiled.

"Well, let's check your blood pressure real fast." I moved so she could get to him. She was so speedy, I could tell she'd done this a gazillion times.

"She looks like you. Skinny," she said, as she put the cuff around Dad's arm.

"Ah, yes, but smart like her mom. Though skinny is handy, because we like to eat a lot," Dad said.

"I like to eat a lot, too." She smiled and pumped the armband. She listened through her stethoscope and scowled at the meter.

"A little low. I'll be back later to check again." The harsh rip of the Velcro from the armband made me jump, and the nurse giggled through her apology, then scurried out as quickly as she'd come in. Dad motioned for me to sit back down, and he put his arm back around me.

"So, how else can I help?" Dad asked.

"I don't know. I just wish I didn't get so scared," I said, rubbing the edge of my T-shirt between my fingers.

"I know this is another repeat, but it does happen to everyone," Dad said.

"But I don't think you've been that scared, really," I said.

"Oh my God, of course I have. When I first got cancer, I was so scared. And the scary thing doesn't just go away ..." Dad paused, and looked up at the ceiling before he continued. "I was reminded recently of something an old teacher of mine once said. 'You can't be brave if you're never afraid' ... but you already know that ..." Dad's voice trailed off. I waited for him to say something else, but I turned and saw his eyes were closing. I shifted to get up, but his arm stiffened.

"Not so fast. I just drifted for a sec."

"It's okay. Do you want to sleep?" I asked.

"No, no. What kind of coach would I be if I zonked out on my girl? I want you leaving here feeling pumped!"

"I'm *sooo pumped,* Dad," I said, trying out sarcasm.

"I know it hasn't been easy, sweetheart." He pulled me in and kissed the side of my head.

"I'd just do better if you were there." I didn't want to make him feel bad, but it just came out. He lifted his hand to my chin, and turned my face toward him.

"That's not true. I didn't get you to finals. You did. You were scared, nervous, whatever you want to call it ... but you found what you needed inside of yourself, and you ran. You did it, Josie. You."

"I suppose," I said, looking down and biting my lip.

"You know there's no place I'd rather be."

"I know. I do."

"I'll be thinking of you the whole time ... like every time. I'm with you every step. And you'll have Mom, and I know Lucas wants to go. You'll get double the enthusiasm with both of them there," he said. He made me realize I wanted her to cheer, with any voice.

"You'll still text me to 'Be fearless,' right?"

"Sure. You don't really need it, but I will." He was squinting and shaking his head. "I am just so proud of you, and how you put yourself out there," he said and kissed my cheek. His eyes were glassy.

"Thanks, Daddy," I smiled.

"I'm feeling a bit dozy, honey. I'm not kicking you out. I just need to close my eyes for a few, but I want to make sure you're good."

"I am. How about you? Do you need another pillow or anything?" I asked, as I got up and pulled his blanket up.

"I'm good," Dad said. "Wait. I need a hug." He sat forward and reached his arms out. I leaned in to hug him.

"I love you," he said as his arms tightened.

"'Cuz I'm so lovable," I replied.

"Yes, you are," he said with a smile.

"I'll let you know how it goes," I added. His eyes were closed by the time I picked up my bag.

While I waited for the elevator, I caught my reflection in the glass. Dad didn't say anything about my eyebrows. I wasn't sure if he didn't notice, or just didn't say. He did say what was important, and before I knew it, I was heading back to his room. Careful not to wake him, I kissed him on the cheek and whispered, "I love you, too, Daddy."

CHAPTER 27

"JOSIE"

Two more minutes, I thought, as I hit snooze and pulled the covers over my shoulder. It didn't feel like a race day. I didn't wake up with that anticipation or excitement, and I didn't feel nauseous, either. I felt like it didn't even matter what shorts I should wear. What was wrong with me?

"Josie? You up?" Mom asked as she came into my room.

"Mmm-hmm."

I felt her sit on my bed, gently leaning against my back.

"How do you feel?"

"Okay," I said, rolling over toward her. She kissed my cheek.

"Oh, your cheek is so snuggy warm. Give me the other

cheek, so it doesn't feel bad I didn't kiss it, too." I turned for Mom to kiss my other cheek. "You want your usual oatmeal? Or maybe a peanut butter and banana shake?"

"Sure. Shmanks, Mom," I said.

"Which one?"

"Both," I said. The shake wasn't part of my usual routine, but it sounded good. Maybe a little change of routine would be okay. I rolled over to check my phone. Two good-luck texts from Bird and Sofia this morning, and "I love you. Be Fearless" from Dad, that he sent late at night.

I opened my drawer to get my lucky blue shorts, and stared at the other colours I had. I held up a bright orange pair, but tossed them back in and grabbed the blue ones. A change in breakfast was one thing, but a change of shorts was too drastic.

After I got dressed, I went downstairs to find Lucas at the dining table, making a poster.

"Mom said I could come to your race!"

"Well, Dad and I talked, and we're so proud of him about the speech, we decided he could miss some school."

"So, look what I'm making! You like the penguin?" he asked, and held up a poster that read, "THIS PENGUIN CAN FLY! GO JOSIE!"

"Aw, nice," I said.

"I promised Dad, if I went to your race, I'd make a fantastic poster. I put 'CHEER FOR JOSIE' on the back, so people behind me will cheer for you, too."

"Thanks, Lucas." I smiled and messed up his hair. He really was as sweet as it was possible to be.

I slid onto the stool, and Mom handed me the bowl of oatmeal and the shake. It was almost as thick as yogurt, so I got a spoon to finish it. Then Mom did my French braids and brow touch-up. It was subtle.

"Maybe without part of my eyebrows, I'll be more aerodynamic."

"Maybe!" Mom laughed. "Come on, let's go!"

■

A disgusting smell greeted us when we drove into the parking lot by the track.

"Yuck! What is that?" Lucas said, pulling his T-shirt up over his nose.

"New tarmac," Mom said. "I don't like that you kids will be breathing this in while you run." My stomach didn't like breathing it in *before* I ran.

"Can I get out here, Mom? Mr. B. and everyone will be in the stands by the 100-metre start line. I'm going to put my stuff down and warm up," I said and hopped out of the car.

I'd heard City Finals were held at a high school known for their sports program, but I didn't expect it to be so big. I walked underneath the stands, as the booming cheers for the 3000-metre runners were in full force above me. I decided to look for Aurora and thank her, before I went to my team, and I also hoped she might give me a last-minute tip. I came out from underneath the bleachers, and saw her by the officials' tent. The butterflies gave their first big surge in my stomach. As I walked over, I stood for a moment, hoping Aurora would see me. And she did.

"Morning. Feeling ready?" she asked, wrinkles framing her warm smile.

"Uh, more like nervous," I said, trying to laugh it off. "I just wanted to thank you for those drills."

"Oh, no thanks necessary. How'd you find it?"

"Hard, but a few times, I felt pretty good about it."

"Well, good for you for trying."

"My dad said, maybe next year I could join a running club. He's a big fan of yours."

"That'd be super! Wait, I have some flyers in here," she said, checking her bum bag, and handing me a small sheet of paper that said, "Flying Eagles Track."

"Oh, thanks."

"All the info is on the website. It's a great group of kids, and you'll like the coaches. And you already know me," she said, with a smile.

"Okay. I'll show my parents."

"Are they here?"

"My mom is. My dad is in the hospital but ..." *But what?* I had nothing to add, but it didn't matter, because someone from the tent was calling her. "Well, I just wanted to say thanks again for helping me." My nose tingled, so I bit my lip. She reached for my hand and squeezed it.

"My pleasure. Now, you have to go run your heart out, and then go tell your dad all about it."

"I will," I said. I took a deep breath as I walked away, and realized that what she said was the same thing I'd been thinking all along.

After I did my warmup, I found Mom and Lucas near the railing by the finish line.

"Hi," Mom said, sounding surprised.

"Hi."

"Everything all right?" she asked.

"Yeah. I didn't get my lucky Mommy kiss," I said, tipping my cheek toward her.

"Oh, of course! How could I forget?" She kissed me. "Give me the other cheek. We don't want it to be upset!"

"I'll take one from you, too. I need all the help I can get," I said to Lucas, and leaned down. He bonked me in the head with the rolled-up poster.

"Ow! Knock me out, why don't you!" I said, and we laughed.

"When is your race?" Lucas asked.

"Why? Are you bored already?"

"No, just ... Mom said I can have a Freezie after you race, and I don't want them to run out of blue."

"Oh," I laughed. "It's supposed to be at eleven. I doubt they'll run out of Freezies."

"You feel okay with that tarmac smell, honey?" Mom asked.

"I can't really smell it anymore," I said.

"Okay, good. One more kiss," Mom said. When I leaned into her, my bag slipped off my shoulder.

"Whoa!" I wobbled as Mom caught me.

"I've got you," she whispered, and hugged me a little

tighter. "You'll do great, my love," she said, and kissed my head, like she always did.

"Thanks, Mom, I kind of have to go now."

"Oh, I know," she chuckled and let go of me. "Just trying to think if I should say anything else. Well, I love you. Now go!"

"You, too. And, Mom ... you think you can be extra loud?"

"You know it," she said, smiling.

"Good luck, Josie," Lucas said. "And don't forget, 'Be fearless.'" He lifted his hand for a high-five.

"Cornball," I said as I slapped it, and bounced through the stands to the area where we were being marshalled.

I got lane 5. Prosciutto and Whippet were on inside lanes. Our hellos were friendly. Everything seemed normal on the way to the start line, but a little abnormal, too. I had the predictable butterflies, heard people calling out from the stands, and spotted Mom at the railing with the sign in front of her—smiling, waving, thumbs up, not at all embarrassing. Lucas stood with Mom's phone in front of him, ready to record. What made it seem so weird and abnormal, was being worried about Dad. The unknown made me feel like time was passing in a different way. Like I was floating outside myself. Did anyone else have this other stuff? Maybe. Probably. And I figured if they could put it aside for a minute and a few seconds, to just run, I could do that, too.

I stretched in my lane, and jumped up and down a few times, noticing a slight springiness in the new track. I shook my hands to get rid of the tension. The crowd quieted. I looked over at Aurora, stepping up on her Ms. Starter platform. The announcer spoke as I put my feet in the blocks. I shifted the tip of my spike slightly, until it felt right. ***Channelling butterflies to my feet, Dad.***

"On your mark ..."

I looked down.

"Get set ..."

I breathed in.

Be fearless.

CHAPTER 28

"TITANIUM"

Launch ...

My feet sensed the horn. Legs charged. I passed two girls out of the curve. Straightened along the track. Breathing hard. I should've settled in but couldn't let up. Prosciutto and the Whippet came alongside.

Push ...

I chased them. Coming around the bend, there was nipping at my heels. Pounding feet were all around me. Pounding was everywhere. I had to get away from that sound.

Drive ...

Some fell back. I was almost there. My lungs pressed up to my chest. I was chasing one; another was chasing me. My legs were fighting me, heavy. I pumped my arms. *Come on, come on!* Seconds away. Panting. I leaned forward, head down, into the finish. I flailed as I slowed down and dropped to my knees. My hands and knees felt the roughness of the track, as my heart banged the top of my ribcage. No clue what place I came in, but I did it. *I did it, Daddy!*

An official helped me up and told us to stay in our lanes. I squeezed my side and saw Mom and Lucas, his skinny arms in the air, and Mom with her hands up to her mouth like a bullhorn. When I waved and smiled, she held up one finger then two, and then both hands. First or second? Really? I did a kind of shrug, and she flashed more fingers and a thumb. *What the heck are you doing?* I thought. I just needed to breathe. Mom clapped above her head, and I could tell she was shouting "Woo!" I bit my lip as I smiled.

The officials led us off the track, and put six of the runners in order. Prosciutto and the Whippet got third and fourth. They told the other girl and me to go sit with the others until they could "figure out what's what." I looked over at Aurora, but she was focused on the next race. Not that I really expected her to wave or do anything.

As we changed out of our spikes, I heard the word "tie" from the group of six sitting nearby. I thought about what Aurora had said, "Run your heart out and go tell your dad." I definitely had something to go back to tell Dad, now. I'd given it my all. That was what mattered. That was something good to tell him.

I sat up on my knees to look for Mom. Her eagle eyes were locked on me, probably waiting for my one-two sign language mash-up. I gave her a flickering wave. She blew me a kiss. I couldn't hear anything during the race, but I hoped she was extra loud.

CHAPTER 29

"ANYTHING COULD HAPPEN"

Mr. B. was holding his goatee as he walked across the field. I put my water bottle in the drawstring bag with my spikes and got up. He was smiling, but as he got closer, I could see his smile was off, like when you bite into a dill pickle and find out it's a sweet one. I knew then it wasn't a tie, and figured coming in second was way better than the disappointment of a sweet pickle.

"I didn't win, did I?" I asked with my arms folded, feeling the spikes through the bag on my hip.

"Aw, Tomaselli, I'm sorry about this, kid," he said.

"It's okay," I smiled, knowing Dad would still be ecstatic that I came second. He put a hand on my shoulder.

"No, no ... I'm sorry to tell you this. You stepped on the line. You've been disqualified." He gave my shoulder a squeeze as it sunk in.

"I ... what?" I snapped, backing away from him. I turned to where Mom and Lucas were standing, but I couldn't see them.

"It really sucks, kid."

"That's impossible!" I could not believe what I'd heard.

"I know. I didn't believe it, either."

"So, where? Where'd I do it?"

"Coming around the last curve. The official said you stepped on the line with your left foot," Mr. B. said, putting his hands on top of one another, like one hand was the line and the other was my foot.

"That's crap!" I whipped my bag toward the curve, but it flung back, and the spikes pierced my elbow through the fabric. I yelped and let go. The bag flopped on the ground in defeat. I wanted to join it on the grass as I felt the tears, but anger kept me standing. Mr. B. picked up the bag and handed it back to me.

"Can't you do something?"

"That's what I've been doing, fighting them on it.

It's not like you interfered with another runner or got a faster time ... but rules are rules, and that old geezer would not budge."

"This is so unfair! I have never, ever stepped on a line. It's all such ... bull!" I choked on the swear. A minute earlier, I had a great story that would've made Dad so happy. I needed that version of the story, not the one I had.

"It sucks, kid, and I am truly sorry."

"I just can't believe this," I said, feeling my eyes well up. The cheering from the stands made my temples pulse, and I wiped my eyes.

"Josie, you put it all out there and had an amazing race. You've got so much to be proud of. And your parents will be proud." I knew he was trying, but I couldn't get past it. I was not second, not last, not even the dreaded fourth. No place.

"Come on, let's go," he said, and put his arm around my shoulder. We walked along the edge of the field to cross over the track.

Mom and Lucas were waiting on the other side of the track, looking as upset as I probably did. When the track was clear, I jogged across to Mom, and just put my head on her shoulder and cried, while Mr. B. came over and filled her in. Lucas was quiet, but I felt the softness of his hands on my fingers. When Mr. B. left, Mom shifted both arms like a cushion around me. Her shoulders muffled my sobs.

"Oh, honey, I am so sorry," Mom said, her voice scratchy from shouting. "I don't know what I can say, except how incredibly proud I am."

"You were really good, Josie," Lucas said, hugging the side of me.

"Thanks," I said, and wiped my eyes. Mom kissed my forehead and put one arm around Lucas. A pang hit my gut, when I thought again about having to tell Dad.

"I'm so tired. Can we just go home and see Dad later?" Mom shook her head nervously, her eyes welling up.

"We should go," she said, her chin starting to quiver. She looked at Lucas and back at me, as she stroked his hair. "I got a call from the hospital. We have to go there now."

CHAPTER 30

"RUNNING TO STAND STILL"

The sound in the room had changed. I didn't need Mom's details about the blood clot, or how he might look, to know what was happening. The noise coming from Dad told me. He gurgled. It was the sound of life vanishing.

Mom went straight to him like he was awake.

"Hey Max," she whispered, and touched his arm. She leaned in toward him. "Massimo ... we're all here." She had her arm around Lucas and ushered him closer. Lucas took Dad's hand, like he didn't need to think about it, or be told where he needed to be. My nose stung, and I bit my bottom lip to hold back the tears.

"He can hear you, honey, if you want to say something,"

Mom said softly to Lucas.

"I'm thinking," Lucas said.

"You take your time, and I'll tell Daddy about Josie's race until you're ready," Mom said, and Lucas nodded his head. Mom took a deep breath in, and forced a smile before she spoke. "It was amazing. You'd have gone wild. She ran like ... no, she flew ..." Mom let out what sounded like a squeak. "Oh, I don't know what I'm saying. Honey, you come tell him about it," Mom said to me.

"And say what?" I mumbled, and stared down at the folded blanket over his feet, perfectly straight and smooth.

"Anything." She stepped aside to make room for me, but I didn't move. Her smile was tight, and her eyes were teary. The gurgling from Dad's slack mouth seemed louder and erratic. I sat, pushing the chair back with my legs, and it scraped the floor.

"I know it's hard," Mom said.

"I can talk to him now," Lucas said. I didn't know if he really was ready, or if he did it for me, but I was relieved and grateful at the same time.

"Um ... hi, Daddy. Sorry we didn't get here before you fell asleep." Lucas sniffed as Mom held him next to her.

"... I ... um, I think the thing I really want to tell you is, I'm going to try to remember everything we did together. As much as I can. I'm even going to write stuff down, just in case. So don't worry, I won't forget you. I think that's all, Mom," he said and grabbed onto Mom. She kissed the top of Lucas's head and wiped her eyes.

"Josie, honey? It'd be good for him to hear you, and good for you, too." I stood and took her outstretched hand.

"I feel ... weird," I said. I didn't know what to say and I just didn't want to talk with them there. I sure wasn't as open or comfortable as Lucas. "Mom, do you think you could go into the hall? Would that be okay?" I asked. Mom took a minute to answer, and her expression made me think she wouldn't go.

"Sure. If that's what you want."

"I do."

"All right, honey. And if you get stuck, tell him about the race. Let's go get something to drink, Lucas." She kissed me and took Lucas's hand. Lucas looked over his shoulder at me with every step.

Alone with Dad. The lights. The screens. I wanted to look anywhere but his face. It seemed stupid, talking to him while he was so out of it, but sitting there felt stupid, too.

"So ..." I slid the chair forward, thinking I should hold his blotchy hand, but settled on the bedside railing instead.

"So, yeah," I said quietly. "Um, the race was ... intense." *Intense? What the hell was I saying?* I'd talk him through it, like Mom said.

"So, I didn't have such a great start, just went flat out. *Fearless,* right?"

"Um ... anyway, I chased the girl in the lead, and there was another girl I could feel on me ... but I caught the lead girl. At the finish I ..." I stammered.

I left him hanging, like how the race had ended for me. Hanging, just like I was now, not knowing what to do, or what would come after this. Could he really even hear me? Dad made this sucking-in sound that made me look at him, mouth still open, his hair stuck to his forehead. His exhale rattled. I slipped my fists under my thighs and held my breath, until his steady gurgle came back.

"So ... at the finish ..." I wanted to make the end of the race different, to tell him I won or came second. I looked at the veins on his hand, bulging, overlapping, and got up and walked behind the chair. Like it would somehow protect me.

"I was disqualified. There!" I clenched the top of the chair and rocked on my feet.

"The idiot official ..." My eyes filled. "That old, senile, jackass! He said I stepped on the line. I have *never* stepped on a line! You know that!" I cried and slapped the chair. The tears wouldn't stay in anymore.

"Being fearless really worked, didn't it, Daddy? I tried like you told me! And then I got disqualified! You didn't tell me this would happen, with you ... you, being like this! Why didn't you tell me?" I pushed the chair, and it made such a loud skidding sound, I checked to see if it had startled him, but he hadn't moved. *Stupid, stupid!* Like it was going to scare him awake?

The St. Peregrine card was up against a vase of flopping flowers. I picked it up and scanned words like "faithful servant," and "hands of God." Did he pray to this guy? And why weren't his prayers answered? It all seemed so pointless.

I leaned on the bed railing, with the card in my hand. *It's just me. No saint coming to help.* I wiped my cheek and took Dad's hand. It was as cool as the metal railing under my arms.

"Come on, Daddy!" I whispered. "Please wake up. Please

try. Squeeze, if you hear me. Isn't that what people say to do?" I sobbed.

"You were supposed to be there for me! And now ... what am I supposed to do now?" I spat out the words, tossing the saint card. I couldn't talk anymore, or stand there, listening to his non-breathing. I didn't know what to do with myself. I ran out of the room, past the nurses' station. I slammed the elevator button, but couldn't wait, and just ran to the stairs. Mom called my name as I leapt down the steps. I couldn't help it—I had to get out.

CHAPTER 31

"BE STILL"

The voices from the hospital pushed me. I sidestepped around people until I got outside. Then I ran. I couldn't stop. To stop meant the worst was going to happen.

I almost stopped at the fountain, where the trails crossed, but I kept running. I almost cut straight through the park to go home, but my feet carried me where I had to go. I ran from the path onto the grass, toward the hill, where the eagle statue perched at the top, waiting.

You got me running, I thought, as I looked down at the blur of the green, and blotches of packed brown mud. I kept talking to Dad in my head, like I was still next to him. *You made me love this. You were the clown and the coach. How can this be happening to me? To us!*

"No!" I cried, the word lodged in my throat, choking me. No one was around to hear me. No one who knew I was losing everything important. Losing the one who believed in me the most. I couldn't fight the sputtering sound that broke from me, the sting in my eyes. The tears weakened me, and I swayed, groaning with each step.

My thighs ached and I was out of breath, but I was almost at the eagle. "I'm on you," Dad used to say, as we neared the top. He said it to poke and prod me. It made me laugh and push harder. "I'm on you" meant it was the final stretch, and he was right there with me, close. I turned, wanting to see him, out of breath behind me, but I only heard my own gasping for air. I was alone on the hill. I would always be alone, and that hollow terror chased me. It was right behind me all the way from the hospital, and I couldn't outrun it. My chest tightened. *Please don't leave me.*

I collapsed at the base of the statue. I wiped my nose, and then wiped my hand on my shirt. I looked up at the tarnished green eagle, its wings arched and ready. I sat against the granite base. It was as cool as Dad's hand.

This was our finish line. It had always been a good

place. Even the last time, when I ran up alone, I felt a sense of accomplishment. I met Aurora and had things to look forward to. *But now what?* How would I do any of it? I put my head between my knees. My breathing slowed but felt heavy, as if the eagle's wing was pressing down on me. I wiped my nose again, and started picking pieces of grass off the side of my running shoes. The shiny black shoes of the policeman, the night of the fair, flashed in my head. I remembered the ambulance, the paramedics, Bird and Sofia. They'd looked so sad, as I talked through my tears.

"I know he's going to die this time."

"I can't be without my dad."

"What am I going to do?"

The words from the fair were my reality. What was I going to do? What did anyone do? *Be fearless?* How was that even possible? That phrase helped, when Dad said it to me before a race, but *this* wasn't something a playlist would get me through. It was Dad who talked me through those races. He didn't think my nerves or fear were stupid. Dad understood. I just didn't think I could do it alone. Not races, and not this.

■

I wiped my cheeks and stood up, wiggled my ankles around. I never really was fearless. Maybe I never would be. I was afraid before every race, but the fear always disappeared by the end. Gone. I was running too hard to notice when it vanished, though. So strange how that happened. Maybe that was it. The horn blew and I ran. I didn't think about the fear. I ran through it. Every race. Every time.

I looked out toward the city. Dad always pointed out a landmark, or a place that had meaning to him. Downtown was straight ahead, and I tried to find the building he worked in, but the truth was, I never paid that much attention. Over to the right was a stretch of trees, with apartment buildings popping through, where Dad grew up. He used to run, and walk his dog, along a trail that led to the ravine. I couldn't remember the name. The view always looked the same to me, but I knew it would never really be the same. I eventually looked left, where there were lush, beautiful trees between the bottom of the hill and the hospital. Only one part of the hospital stuck out from the cluster of trees, as if to wave. *I don't have to go there anymore.* Did it make me a bad person for thinking that?

Standing against the statue, I realized I *did* have to go back. Mom and Lucas were probably still there, and I knew they'd be worried. Lucas was probably confused. The last thing I wanted was for him to feel lost. I felt a sting in my eyes, just thinking about Lucas, how he was when we were in the garage, how he was going to be. I had to be there for him.

I started walking down the hill, and thought about what Dad had said, about how grateful he was for his friends. They went through a lot together, and helped make him who he was. He needed them, like I needed Bird and Sofia. I knew they'd be there for me, not just because they told me, but because that's just how it had always been. And it went both ways. I had to be there when they needed me, too. We took turns, like Sofia said.

I didn't know what I would do when I got back to the hospital. I told myself I didn't have to go into Dad's room, if I didn't want to. My stomach lurched. Dad in the bed. Me yelling at him and running away. I was scared of *him*. That wasn't Dad, though. Dad ran with me. Dad made me laugh. Dad hugged me all the time. Sometimes too much. He thought I could do anything. Believed in me. He showed his pride every time he smiled. He saw me. I needed to get back to see him. To tell him I loved him.

I let gravity tug me into a jog. The real fear hadn't been with me at the top of the hill. Fear was back at the hospital. But Dad didn't mean I had to be without fear, he meant I had to face it, to run through it. I'd done it before, and would have to do it again. I had to get back. I needed him to know I would be okay, and that I understood. I started to run.

ACKNOWLEDGMENTS

Ask anyone who knows me, and they'll agree that brevity isn't my thing. And when gratitude is sprinkled in, I struggle to find the right words. Please forgive the rambling.

I kind of want to thank anyone who ever listened to my chapters at Mabel's Fables from 2012 onward, but that'd be silly. The core, though, the ones I could not have done it without: Carol, Rob, Ann, Christin, Tori, Michael, Richard, Jenn, and Kim. Our get-togethers outside class, your ideas and talent, helped make my story and my writing better. Or, at least, not so "tepid." I've been thanking Ted Staunton since March 2020, even though his impact on me goes back to 2012. As our fearless leader, he detects nuances and shares insights that leave me amazed. I'm so grateful to him for raking through my manuscript, raising questions, offering suggestions, and giving encouragement. I still have far to go. Thank you. Again.

I'll never know how I got so lucky for my first book to be under the editorial guidance of Beverley Brenna at Red Deer Press. Many people have only ever "met" over email or zoom during COVID, but I think it's additionally screwy that our connection formed through run-ons, bad grammar, and misused punctuation. I am ever thankful to Beverley for making this process so smooth (from my end), and, dare I say, fun! One day, I hope to meet for coffee and some Italian pastries.

After eight years, and an unknown number of versions and rewrites, I bravely let my family and a few friends have a look. So, to those "early" readers: my famjam, Mom, Joey, Kelly, Dana, Beth, Michele and Erin—thank you for all your input and for being that safe space. I also appreciate the group of "later" readers, whose feedback and support meant so much. I took it all in.

When memories are fuzzy or absent, sometimes it's just the feelings that stick. I'm fortunate to have grown up where I did, and I tried to drizzle in a little love for my childhood friendships. So, for all we ran through together: Heather, Sue, Patty, MariaElena, Karen, Dina, Esther, and Amy. Thanks for helping to raise me.

My final ramble is to my family. My Mommy, Barbara: I'm so lucky to have you as my biggest cheerleader. I share nostalgia with my generous brother Joey, though it's his memory I rely on. My stepfather, Al, along with my aunts and cousins, who always embraced the goofy in me. My tripod—Rafe, Allegra, and Lincoln—you make my heart burst. You've given me so much material for this story, and tolerated my sharing—but let's face it, I've given you plenty to tease me about. I figure we're even. And to Shaun, il mio primo, il mio ultimo, il mio tutto.

Photo credit: Shaun Osborne

INTERVIEW WITH
LORIE SCARFAROTTI

When did you start writing this debut novel, and how has it changed through the revision process?

The story changed even before the revision process! I started writing it in April 2012, when I joined the Writing for Children Workshop through George Brown College. I'd love to say I had a beautiful outline, but really, I only had a vague idea, and no clue how to get there. My original first chapter was the one when Josie shaved the ends of her eyebrows (Chapter 23, "Hiccup"). I wrote about a dozen more chapters, and when I finished the chapter called "Run," it felt more like a "launching off" point, a better first chapter than "Hiccup." I read it in the workshop, and everyone agreed. So, then I was in a real pickle! My timeline was a mess, the sequence of events shifted, and there were a lot of holes I needed to fill. I added new chapters, read pieces in class, and rewrote things several times, before I could move forward. When I finally did reach the end, I had the framework of what "happened" in the story, but I needed to make it better. That was when the hard work started!

In *Running Through It*, you pull us very realistically into the life of thirteen-year-old Josie Tomaselli. As an adult author writing for young people, how do you create authentic situations for your characters, without sentimentality or nostalgia? Are there cultural aspects of the book that connect to your real life?
Oh, right—I'm an adult! I forget at times, then someone calls me "Mommy!" I have three kids, and I admit that I have snatched material from them. (Josie's fast hair and lucky shorts, Lucas's Scrabble speech). For many years, I volunteered at their schools in various clubs, so I was around a lot of kid chatter. I usually start with the dialogue, and try to imagine being present with the characters, often in a more playful state of mind. In contrast, I feel

sentimentality and nostalgia are much more "adult," especially when looking back at something. I definitely pulled from my real life, especially my Italian side, when it came to food. Food, or rather feeding, was an act of love. One situation I put in the story was when Josie remembers her grandmother giving her a bowl of tomato sauce with bread. My beloved Aunt Mary would do that for me, but I had to try to write it as Josie's memory, without my own sappy sentimentality. (I really did jiggle her arms, too!)

During the week this story unfolds, we see Josie as a Track & Field competitor, running the 400-metre in a city championship. Her fictional story contains detailed, active scenes related to racing. How did you research this aspect of your story, in order to make it come alive? Were there any other parts of the story that required in-depth research?

My kids all used to run, so I spent a lot of time at cross-country and track meets. My daughter was the most serious about it, and belonged to a club from Grades 7 to 12, so most of my "research" comes from that time period. She would help me when I got stuck, or needed to get the feeling right. I also have a photo of her hand, with the times her coach had given her, so I got that "first hand." I did have to read up and watch a few videos on setting up starting blocks, though!

I also did some research on lung cancer recurrence, although it was way over my head. A doctor friend and classmates helped me, based on their work and experiences. I'd also visited a friend in the hospital, so some of that imagery was painfully fresh. Finding a balance of what details to put in or leave out was hard. I didn't want the story to be about Dad's illness. It didn't matter what he had, what was central was how Josie would deal with it. By focusing on what Josie experienced and picked up on, I hoped that would be what took the reader away.

What made you want to anchor this book in such powerful themes of grief and loss, related to the illness of Josie's father?

When my mother was moving, she gave me a box of my junk that had my old diary in it. It's full of cringe-worthy crushes, but the thing that struck me the most, was that there was hardly any mention of my father, who died at the end of that year. I was fourteen. By the accounts in my diary, I was more concerned with what boy smiled at me.

My memories of that time are patchy; I don't remember feeling afraid, or any meaningful conversations. The realization and fear did bubble up one night at a fair, however. All this to say, it made me very curious about how children cope with the "biggest everything," like parental illness, and it's what drove me to explore it, not knowing where it would lead. And while the story is about loss, hopefully the elements of love come through as well.

One of the messages Josie's Dad gives her is the advice to "be fearless." Is this a message you also want to convey to your readers, and in what contexts might it apply?
I wish I remembered how I came up with that phrase! I didn't set out for it to be a message, but I wanted Dad to say something to help Josie combat her nerves before a race. As the story grew, I kept wondering about the various meanings there would be for Josie. Did it mean to have no fear? Was that possible? What had Josie learned about fear, like after a race was over? I suppose readers might see it as a message, that we all experience fear, and it can come in many forms. It can be anticipating something we are about to do, like run a race, or give a speech. It can be unexpected or unimaginably scary. Another message

could be that fear comes and goes; sometimes we can ride it out on our own, but most times, we need people we love, and who love us, to help us through it.

One of the unique aspects of this book is Josie's "playlist"— the songs she and her dad have pulled together to help her train, and which become chapter titles of this novel. Were these songs always part of Josie's story? How did you collect them and embed them in this narrative?
This was such fun! I knew early on that Josie would listen to music when she went out for a run. I also thought it'd be a good way for her to distract herself from being nervous before a race. When I wrote "Run," I kept remembering a line in "Autumnsong" by Manic Street Preachers that Josie would identify with, so I included that right away. I went through music on my phone and added "Dog Days Are Over" to inspire her to run fast for her father. I asked one of my sons for ideas ("Middle Distance Runner") and broadened the net, thanks to Google. I was reminded of so many old songs, and that's when I figured Dad had to get in on the action! I imagined the bantering between him and Josie, and even Mom butting in with disco suggestions! The list I compiled was pretty long, and I eventually chose songs

that, in my mind, either Josie or Dad would like. Pairing song titles to chapters was one of the last things I did. I read what was happening in each chapter, and thought about how a song would relate. Sometimes it was only one line, a message for Josie, a sentiment from Dad, or the tone of a chapter. I started with "Run" and ended with "Be Still," for their special meaning for each scene, but really, a lot of them are pretty special! Go back and take a look!

This story has captivating moments that deal with "secrets." What made you so conscious of the potential that secrets have in creating engaging scenes?

I have a feeling my answer will be slightly disappointing, because I wasn't all that conscious! I just knew some things needed to be hidden, or come out slowly, in an attempt to bring the reader along with Josie as she discovered things. We all keep things hidden or private … maybe out of embarrassment, or protection, or it's just easier to avoid it … like when Josie shaved the ends of her eyebrows, or how Dad had never mentioned that he smoked. I'm sure readers clue in before Josie does about Dad's condition, and will understand when the truth comes "out of its hiding place," like she says in Chapter 21. Hopefully, learning about what makes the characters tick, in this way, does engage readers in the story.

What advice do you have for other writers—young or old—to support them in their craft?

The advice I have is based on what was given to me: Write! It doesn't have to be a masterpiece (clearly!)—but just keep going, and it'll get there. If you get stuck, there are some great prompts out there. Prompts keep you writing, and you never know what might come out (my "Little Giant" chapter is the result of a writing prompt). Read whatever genre is of interest to get a handle on what's out there. It might be out of people's comfort zone, but I'd suggest finding a writing group of some kind. I learned not only from comments about my own story, but from listening to others' work, hearing ideas and questions that were raised, and thinking about aspects of my work I'd previously missed. Basically, just keep writing ... and go for it!

In other words, Be Fearless! Thank you, Lorie, for writing such an inspirational book.